"Your sons are very caring and kind and wonder...wonderful." Violet's voice quivered and she drew in a deep breath before she continued. "You're very lucky to have them."

"That's what everyone told me after Brie died." He looked up at the afternoon sky, the sun starting to make its way closer to the Teton mountain range. "How lucky I was to still have a piece of her."

"No, I meant you're lucky to have them period. Even if your wife was still here, I would tell you the same thing. Your children are a blessing. You're a very fortunate man, Marcus. Not everyone will get to have that same experience, let alone twice."

His heartbeat stopped before picking up speed. "Back at the church, right before you, uh...threw up... you seemed really surprised that I had twins."

She tilted her head and narrowed her eyes at him, as though the answer should have been obvious. "Because *we* were supposed to have twins. There were two babies when I miscarried."

Marcus's knees buckled and his hand propped against the hood of the SUV was the only thing that kept him from going down.

* * *

TWIN KINGS RANCH: A homecoming to remember...

Dear Reader,

When I ventured out of my fictional town of Sugar Falls to start the new Twin Kings Ranch series, there was one character I couldn't leave behind. Freckles, the owner of the Cowgirl Up Café, has a big personality and dispenses advice as quickly as she dispenses hot buttermilk biscuits. She's almost like a fairy godmother of sorts, but with way more sass, formfitting clothes and hair spray.

My own godmother is a lot like Freckles in that she always shows up. Aunt Bonnie (who is technically my mom's cousin) rarely misses a baby shower, a birthday party, a graduation or even a funeral. She is not only front and center with a side dish and a happy smile, she's usually behind the scenes, as well—organizing the meals, assisting with the planning and giving rides to the aunties or whoever else needs a lift. Aunt Bonnie might not match Freckles when it comes to eyeshadow layers, but she definitely brings the fun-loving attitude and the sage advice.

In *Not Their First Rodeo*, Marcus and Violet finally get a chance to have their story told. And just like the first two books in the Twin Kings Ranch series, Freckles is showing up for the King family with her comfort food, her matchmaking skills and her irreverent humor.

For more information on my other Special Edition books, visit my website at christyjeffries.com or chat with me on Twitter at @ChristyJeffries. You can also find me on Facebook and Instagram. I'd love to hear from you.

Enjoy!

Christy Jeffries

Facebook.com/AuthorChristyJeffries

Twitter.com/ChristyJeffries (@ChristyJeffries)

Instagram.com/Christy_Jeffries/

Not Their First Rodeo

CHRISTY JEFFRIES

SPECIAL EDITION™

Recycling programs for this product may not exist in your area.

ISBN-13: 978-1-335-40794-8

Not Their First Rodeo

Copyright © 2021 by Christy Jeffries

For questions and comments about the quality of this book, please contact us at CustomerService@Harlequin.com.

Harlequin Enterprises ULC
22 Adelaide St. West, 40th Floor
Toronto, Ontario M5H 4E3, Canada
www.Harlequin.com

Printed in U.S.A.

Christy Jeffries graduated from the University of California, Irvine, with a degree in criminology and received her Juris Doctor from California Western School of Law. But drafting court documents and working in law enforcement was merely an apprenticeship for her current career in the dynamic field of mommyhood and romance writing. She lives in Southern California with her patient husband, two energetic sons and one sassy grandmother. Follow her online at christyjeffries.com.

Books by Christy Jeffries

Harlequin Special Edition

Twin Kings Ranch

What Happens at the Ranch...
Making Room for the Rancher

Sugar Falls, Idaho

A Marine for His Mom
Waking Up Wed
From Dare to Due Date
The Matchmaking Twins
The Makeover Prescription
A Proposal for the Officer
A Family Under the Stars
The Firefighter's Christmas Reunion
The SEAL's Secret Daughter

Montana Mavericks: What Happened to Beatrix?

His Christmas Cinderella

Visit the Author Profile page at Harlequin.com.

To my own fairy godmother, Bonnie Johnston Holbrook.
You have boundless energy and the biggest heart.
You're the glue that keeps our extended family together
and my heart smiles every time I see you. Thank you for
always showing up (and for always buying my books).
Love you to the moon and back.

Chapter One

Marcus King hated funerals.

As the sheriff of Ridgecrest County in Wyoming, he even avoided traffic details for cemetery processions, often assigning a junior deputy for the task, just so he wouldn't have to deal with the painful reminder that death could happen to anyone at any time. A fact he knew only too well, having lost his wife five years ago.

However, Marcus hadn't been able to avoid this particular memorial service, with thousands of mourners lined up outside the crowded church and millions more at home watching live on their televisions. Celebrities, national heroes and world leaders were all crammed into the too-small First Congregation of Teton Ridge, watching somberly as the president of the United States gave the eulogy for her second-in-command.

Vice President Mitchell "Roper" King had been many things to many people, but to Marcus he'd simply been Dad.

And how did one escape his own father's funeral while hundreds of news cameras were strategically placed both inside and outside the church to capture every tear, every sniffle, every flicker of emotion that crossed the faces of those who had known and loved Roper King the most?

Well, not everyone in attendance felt that way, Marcus thought as he shifted in the tight confines of his pew to angle his head toward the opposite side of the building.

"Stop squirming in your seat," his brother Duke whispered out the corner of his mouth. "You're not five anymore."

"I'm checking on my sons," Marcus replied before giving a curt nod to his twin boys sitting with their younger cousin in the pew behind them. "They've got to be bored out of their minds."

Six-year-old Jordan and Jack were hanging in there like a couple of champs, though. Sad, but hiding their restlessness way better than their old man. Probably because their aunt had promised all the kids doughnuts and brand-new iPads loaded with their favorite video games if they could keep still during the nearly one-hour service.

Marcus glanced past his sons' honey-blond heads to the packed pews behind them and caught a glimpse of the upper corner of a woman's face.

No. That couldn't be...

Surely *she* wouldn't come to the funeral, especially knowing Marcus would be there. He craned his neck to get a better look and felt his brother's elbow ram directly into the cold piece of steel secured in place below his rib cage.

Duke stifled a curse, and their mother gave them both a withering stare through her sheer black veil. When she returned her attention to the president speaking in front of the flag-draped casket, Duke muttered, "Did you seriously wear your duty holster to the service?"

"I always wear it," Marcus said, tugging on the lapels of his uncomfortable suit. "Just in case something comes up and I need to respond to a call."

"You're allowed to take the day off."

Yet Marcus never took time away from work. At least, not mentally. This was his home, his county. These people, most of them visitors, were ultimately his responsibility until they all returned to their own worlds. He glanced down at his watch. Hopefully, that would be in less than fifteen more minutes. They just needed to get through the video montage and then the procession before he could—

"Where's Tessa going?" His brother nodded to where their sister was rushing down the center aisle toward the small vestibule that led to the front doors.

"I'll go check." Marcus began to rise, but his mother, who was on his opposite side, quickly shot her arm across his midsection, just like she used to do when she'd driven him to school or baseball practice and had to slam on the brakes.

"Don't you dare stand up and cause a bigger scene." She spoke quietly, but firmly. "We have people stationed outside who can see to her."

The Secret Service agent positioned in the shadows behind the organ put his hand over the clear wire of his earpiece. Marcus had attended the pre-op briefing earlier today with several deputies from his department, as well as numerous other law-enforcement personnel from neighboring counties. Right now, he would've given anything to know what was being transmitted over the radio communications. The agent made eye contact with Marcus and gave a very discreet thumbs-up before resuming his stance.

Which meant he had to stay put and actually deal with the grief of losing his father. Instead of thinking about something simple like logistics and security perimeters, he had to think about how much he was going to miss seeing his dad's proud, but crooked smile. How he was never going to hear that rugged, but reassuring voice give him any more words of advice. Damn it. Marcus wanted to mourn in private, on his own schedule. Certainly not in front of a crowd.

The final ten minutes of the ceremony seemed to last longer than the first fifty, but finally the pallbearers, consisting of members of each branch of the armed services, carried the casket down the center aisle. His mother followed, supported by the president who'd been sitting in the front pew on the opposite side. That left Marcus to walk next to the first gentleman while mourners nodded their condolences at them as they passed each row.

If there was anything Marcus avoided more than funerals, it was politicians. Sure, the president and her husband were polite enough, and his father had made numerous friends with elected officials and cabinet members over the years. But there were plenty of people who'd traveled all the way to Roper King's small hometown in the middle of Wyoming just for the opportunity to be seen rubbing elbows with some of the most powerful leaders in the country.

Like the senior senator from the great state of Texas. And wherever Senator Cortez-Hill went, her famous husband followed, causing even more of a stir with his celebrity status as a member of the Baseball Hall of Fame.

Perfect. The only thing that would make this day even more unbearable was if they'd brought…

Oh, hell. There she was.

Violet Cortez-Hill.

Marcus's lungs seized, and his knees threatened to buckle as his eyes locked on hers. It *had* been her sitting way back here, after all. And she was even more beautiful than she'd been the last time he'd seen her—almost fourteen years ago. Her black hair was still silky straight, but slightly shorter, and framed her heart-shaped face. Her light bronze complexion still smooth and flawless, and her narrow nose still regal. But her cheekbones were sharper and more defined, and her green eyes held more wisdom and cynicism. His gaze flickered lower to her lips, which were drawn tight, as though she was holding her breath as she boldly returned his stare.

He should've listened to his instincts earlier and volunteered for traffic detail. Funerals didn't just force people to publicly confront their grief and their own invincibility. They often forced people to confront mistakes from their pasts. And now he was face-to-face with his.

Why had Violet come? Didn't she know how uncomfortable this would be for all of them?

A hand clasped his shoulder and propelled him forward.

"Keep on moving, Lover Boy," Duke grunted from behind. Marcus hadn't heard the nickname in years, and instead of sending him on a trip down memory lane, it immediately snapped him back to the present.

Putting one foot in front of the other, he squared his shoulders and followed the procession down the aisle, outside the church and into the bright January sunshine and the even brighter lights of the news cameras. He shoved his dark sunglasses on just in time, once again wishing he could be anywhere but here.

As the casket was loaded into the back of the hearse, he felt the small hands of his boys, each on one side, taking his bigger palms in theirs. Marcus couldn't afford to think about anything but taking care of his children, being the support that they needed through the devastating loss of another family member. He'd told his children that it was okay to cry, that it was okay to be sad. They'd both been so young when their mother had died, their grieving process had been somewhat delayed. As though they'd known they were missing something but didn't quite understand who or what until later. Losing their beloved grandfather, though, had the potential to stir up all sorts of feelings they'd yet to deal with about their mom's death.

Marcus's dad had once been his rock, and now more than ever he was determined to provide the same stability to his own sons.

"Where's Aunt Tessa?" Jordan whispered, concern permanently etched across the serious boy's brow. "She left real quick, and her face was all white."

"Maybe she was hungry and wanted to get something to eat," Marcus replied, doubting the excuse before he even said it.

"Well, I have to go pee, and I don't think I can hold it," Jack announced much louder. Despite being older by three minutes, Jack was the free-spirited twin. The impulsive one that counterbalanced his brother's tendency to worry about every little thing. "She better not eat all the sprinkle doughnuts before we get there."

Marcus bit back a groan, yet he couldn't help but also feel a sense of relief. His sons were actually handling the funeral crowd much better than expected. Being a single father, he'd dealt with plenty of tears and tantrums in the past and knew it came with the territory. Today, though, he'd much rather deal with doughnuts and bathroom breaks.

He squeezed their hands and said, "Let's go back inside and use the restroom. Then we'll go see if they have any more snacks left in the MACC staging tent."

In fact, it felt good to have something concrete to focus on, to have a task at hand. Plus, it didn't hurt that his sons' requests gave him the perfect excuse to get away from everyone in the crowd and check on his sister all at the same time. While he was there, he could ask his deputies stationed in the Multi-Agency Command Center temporarily set up behind the building if they needed anything from him.

Marcus chanced a glance behind him at the guests spilling onto the church steps to see if anyone was watching them, then told his kids, "Come on. Let's hop over those bushes by the sidewalk and double back to the side door. It'll be the quickest way."

It would also be the only route that guaranteed

he didn't come face-to-face with the woman who'd made him stop in his tracks earlier.

The woman who used to hold his heart in the palm of her hand.

Violet Cortez-Hill knew when she'd landed at Jackson Hole Airport it would only be a matter of time before she'd see Marcus King, the man who'd once been her best friend and her first love.

Everyone probably would have understood why she couldn't find time to attend the funeral in Wyoming. But she was in between high-profile cases right now, and after fourteen years, it felt cowardly to use work as an excuse just to hide behind all those emotions that belonged in the past. And nobody had ever accused Violet of being a coward.

Besides, she'd spent so much of her adolescent summers with the older King children when their parents had forced them to attend the same political events, and she had adored their father, Roper. How could she not be here to pay her respects in person? To offer any support she could.

Yet, when her eyes had locked on Marcus's during the final procession, she'd been slammed with a million memories. It felt as though a wave had crashed into her, practically knocking her back into the hard, wooden pew.

How was it that he'd grown even more handsome over the years? That his shoulders had gotten broader and his face had gotten more chiseled? The teenager she'd once dated used to wear ripped jeans, T-shirts with goofy slogans and an old ball cap from Dorsey's Tractor Supply. Yet the man who'd stopped in the middle of the aisle to stare at her with openmouthed shock wore an expensive tailored suit and a short, neat haircut, looking nothing like the guy she used to know. Unfortunately, his nearness still caused her pulse to spike with the same level of attraction as it had all those years ago.

His brother Duke had given him a shove and Violet was left to stand there and wonder if the few seconds they'd made eye contact was really long enough for her to conclude that his reaction to seeing her had been just as intense as hers. She fought the urge to rub away the dull ache in her temples, telling herself that Marcus's response was simply due to his surprise.

The church was small and the aisle narrow, so it took ages for the rows in front of them to empty. As the rest of the mourners filed out of the church, Violet whispered to her mother, "I'm going to use the ladies' room."

"Now?" Senator Eva Cortez-Hill said through her teeth as she nodded somberly at the other politicians and A-list celebrities making their way down the aisle. "All the networks have cameras outside, and it would be a great opportunity for you to get some coverage before my next election."

"Mom, we've already been over the fact that I

have no intention of running for superior court judge. Now's not the time to rehash that argument."

"You aren't hoping to run into *you know who*, are you?" After all these years, her mother still couldn't bring herself to say Marcus's name.

"Of course not, Mom. That's all in the past."

"Fine. But be outside in five minutes. Our car will be the third one behind the president's in the motorcade, and the Secret Service won't want to wait."

Violet nodded before going in the opposite direction toward the vestibule hallway that led toward the restrooms. Her family had been in the public eye for as long as she could remember, so the cameras and parades of vehicles and formal appearances were certainly nothing new. Yet, that didn't mean she relished living her life in the spotlight, even if she was good at pretending otherwise. In fact, being a public defender, representing some of the most heinous criminals in the justice system, she'd quickly learned how to mask any facial expressions that might give away how she was truly feeling inside. Every day, she sat beside strangers in orange jumpsuits accused of an array of charges and didn't hesitate to defend their right to a fair trial.

So then, why was she currently ducking into the bathroom of a small church in the middle of Wyoming? Why was she hiding out in a cramped powder room that hadn't had its floral wallpaper or framed cross-stitch decor changed out in at least four decades?

Violet braced her hands on the pink-tiled counter and stared at her reflection over the sink. "Because the last time you saw Marcus King, your world fell apart shortly after."

Her phone vibrated in her purse, and she felt a stinging pressure building behind her eyes, the telltale sign of a migraine coming on. Yanking out her phone, she saw the text from her father asking if she was okay. She fired a quick response.

I'm fine. Go on without me and I'll catch up with you guys later at the airport.

She dug around in her purse for the pills her doctor had prescribed for migraines. Even though taking them made her feel as though she were admitting defeat, she knew that it was smart to stay ahead of the pain and the accompanying nausea before it got worse. Turning on the water, she cupped her hand under the faucet and took a deep drink.

Next, she reapplied her lipstick and tried to ignore how pale her cheeks looked in the fluorescent lights and pink-hued surrounding of the ladies' room. Checking the time on her phone, she convinced herself that the motorcade was likely long gone, hopefully with Marcus in one of the first vehicles. She could slip outside and pretend nothing was amiss.

And then do what?

Ask a reporter for a ride in a news van? Call a cab? Did they have Uber in Teton Ridge? Okay, so maybe this wasn't one of her better thought-out plans. *This* was why she tried not to let her emotions get the better of her.

"C'mon," she told herself in the mirror. There were hundreds of people in attendance at the funeral. Surely someone would be heading her way. "For God's sake, what's with you? You're smart. You're resourceful. You've just been named one of the top litigators in *Lone Star Docket* magazine. Finding a ride to the airport should be the least of your problems. Get it together, damn it."

Finally the pep talk worked. She ran a hand through her dark hair and turned to the door. Straightening her spine, she left the safety of her temporary hideout with her head held high.

Only to slam into the very man she'd been trying to avoid.

Marcus's hands were firm and strong on her shoulders as he caught her, then immediately released her when his surprised face recognized hers.

"Violet." His voice was deeper than she'd remembered, and his solemn tone was definitely less playful. But at least it wasn't accusatory, which might have been how she would've sounded if he'd shown up at her father's funeral.

She drew in a deep breath, trying to ignore his citrus and leather–scented shower gel, still familiar after all these years. "Hi, Marcus. I'm deeply sorry for your loss."

A storm of emotion passed behind those blue eyes

of his, as though fighting to remember why they were both here in the vestibule of the First Congregation of Teton Ridge. Her stomach roiled and twisted in a storm of its own, and she didn't know if it was a symptom from her impending migraine or a symptom of standing inches away from her ex-boyfriend.

Finally, he rubbed the back of his neck before giving her a curt nod. "Thank you."

She wanted to ask him how he was holding up, but the slight shadow of his sunken cheeks told her that he wasn't doing well. The stiff resolve in his square jaw similarly told her that he wouldn't admit it.

Clearly, neither one wanted to be the first to run away from the history between them. She could make an excuse about needing to catch her ride, but what if he followed her outside and saw that everyone had already left?

Speaking of the motorcade, why was he still here? Why hadn't he ridden in the family limos with his mother and siblings? It was on the tip of her tongue to ask him, but he crossed his arms over his chest, his defensive posture suggesting he was more than willing to stand there silently and wait her out.

He reminded her of a court bailiff or a guard at the jail who stood by stoically as she interviewed one of her clients, annoyed by the assignment and pretending not to be counting the minutes until he could be out of her presence.

The longer Marcus remained planted there staring at her, the more her pulse pounded with annoyance. Was he not even slightly curious about what had happened to her? Or at least willing to be polite and pretend he cared?

What made it worse was that Violet desperately wanted to ask him all kinds of questions about *his* life. To find out what he'd been doing since he'd vanished from her life without so much as a *see ya* fourteen years ago.

Yet she doubted he'd be forthcoming with those answers, either. Instead she said, "I saw Tessa leave the service early. I hope she's okay."

Even to her ears it sounded like she was fishing for information rather than simply trying to engage him in conversation. But the alternative would have been to either stand there silently and let the awkward tension build or to dash away as though she had something to hide.

Plus, she had always been fond of Tessa and was legitimately concerned about his sister. Marcus might not be willing to talk about himself, but he'd never been able to hide his concern for his family.

For the first time, his eyes darted away from her, and he cleared his throat. "Tessa wasn't feeling well, and a Secret Service agent took her to the command center tent to have the medics examine her."

"Oh, no. I could go check on her," Violet said, taking a step back. In fact, the migraine medicine wasn't kicking in as quickly as she'd hoped, and the nausea bubbling inside her was growing worse. Having grown up around big events like this, she knew there'd be a staging area behind the church that would be quicker to access on foot. The thought of some fresh air and an anti-nausea pill had her pivoting to leave.

"Actually." His voice was commanding and held the slightest warning. Violet paused midturn as he continued. "I'm going to be heading that way when I get done here. I'll let her know you were concerned."

The subtle, yet presumptive, instruction wasn't lost on Violet. Marcus clearly didn't want her going in the same direction as him. Or maybe he didn't want her having any contact with his family. Which was too bad because the MACC tent was usually staffed with first responders and government employees who would be more than willing to assist her in finding alternate transportation to the airport.

Her neck stiffened with irritation, and she lifted her chin. "In that case, don't let me keep you."

He rocked back on the heels of his expensive leather cowboy boots but didn't make a move to leave. "I'm waiting for someone."

Violet felt the color drain from her face. Had there been someone else in the ladies' room when she'd been in there giving herself a pep talk in the mirror? Was it his wife? She'd inadvertently heard through the political grapevine that he'd married a while ago, but she'd stopped herself from ever confirming the fact. In fact, she'd practically made it a personal mission to avoid any news about Marcus. After their breakup, she'd told herself that she had more important things to focus on and he didn't deserve the headspace. But maybe that had been a mistake. Violet wouldn't go into a courtroom without briefing the relevant facts of the case, so why had she shown up on his home turf so unprepared?

Instead of a wife coming out of the ladies' room, though, the door to the men's restroom sprang open, and two young boys spilled out.

"Jack didn't use any soap when he washed his hands," one of the children quickly said to Marcus.

"That's cuz I finished before Jordan and didn't touch the flusher, Dad."

"Dad?" Violet heard herself squeak as her eyes darted between the identical boys and Marcus. "They're…yours?"

She tried to swallow as a sickening wave threatened to upend the contents of her stomach. She put a hand to her lower abdomen as though she could stop the building discomfort, or at least the ghost of a long-ago pain.

"Yes," Marcus said, putting an arm around each boy as all three sets of matching blue eyes blinked skeptically at her. "These are my sons. Jack and Jordan King. Boys, this is my…uh…an old friend of the family."

"They…" Her throat spasmed, and she waited a beat before trying again. "They're twins."

It was more of a statement than a question. And an accusatory one at that.

"Yes," Marcus replied slowly, one blondish-brown

eyebrow lifting. "Why do you look so shocked? It runs in my family."

She felt the perspiration dotting her upper lip even as a chill raced down her spine.

Because once, *they* were going to have twins.

She almost admitted as much aloud, but she was already shoving her way back through the restroom door, barely making it into the stall before the contents of her stomach tore through her.

Chapter Two

"Hey, lady? Are you okay?"

Violet was shocked to see one of the boys holding the stall door open, watching her closely after she'd finished heaving and flushed the toilet. She was even more shocked to see his twin brother and their father behind him in the cramped confines of the ladies' room.

Marcus must've known how awkward it was for him and his two young sons to have witnessed her indelicate moment, because he said, "You left the door open. Jordan was worried and wanted to come check on you."

She nodded because what else was she supposed to say? *Get out? Leave me alone?* She might've easily been able to say something like that to Marcus, but not to his young sons, who were so obviously concerned about her. Scratch that. One son was obviously worried. The other son peeking out behind his dad's hip was wide-eyed, and his lips were curled down in disgust—as though he, too, might vomit soon.

"Is it a foodborne illness?" The one who must be Jordan asked the question. There was a small crease above his freckled nose as his narrowed eyes assessed her. "Or maybe a viral gastro-testnal infection?"

Violet blinked several times at the child's attempt to use proper medical terms. "Uh, I don't think so."

She delicately stepped around him to make her way to the sink before carefully dipping her head down to rinse out her mouth and splash water on her flushed cheeks. Yet the boy followed her, his serious expression reflected at her in the mirror as she used a paper towel to dry her face.

"Do you have a fever?" he asked. "Or diarrhea?"

"Okay, Doctor Jordan, let's give Miss Cortez-Hill some space," Marcus said as he steered both of his boys toward the door, which was still wide-open. He glanced over his shoulder and told Violet, "Sorry about the intrusion. Jordan's been really into WebMD and those emergency-room documentaries on TV lately. He ran in here before I could stop him."

"Thank you for checking on me," she told the boy. Even with all the humiliation still radiating through her, something tugged at Violet's heartstrings. Of course, she would've preferred some privacy, but she wasn't immune to the concern or the curiosity of the child, who did look pretty worried. Her hand shook slightly as she unwrapped one of the pastel breath mints some nice church lady had set out in a glass bowl on the counter. By the time she reapplied her lipstick—for a second time—her fingers were barely trembling. Her hair and eye makeup were beyond repair, she thought as she gave herself one last look in the mirror, but at least her migraine was already subsiding. The sooner she got away from Marcus and Teton Ridge, the better she would feel.

Unfortunately, that wouldn't be anytime soon. The man and his sons were still there, waiting for her in the empty lobby area. She glanced out the wooden double doors leading to the steps outside and saw that many of the cars and news vans were long gone.

"You're able to walk by yourself so far." Jordan rushed to her side with his hands up, like a pint-size spotter to prevent her from falling down. "That's a good sign."

"I'd probably get dizzy and throw up, too, if I had to walk around in those kinds of shoes." Jack, the other twin, frowned skeptically at Violet's high heels. "Maybe you should just go barefoot."

Violet bit back a smile. "I appreciate everyone's concern, but I'm fine now. I promise. I just get these little headaches every once in a while, and they make my tummy unhappy."

"Those are called migraines," Jordan said with confidence. "Our teacher gets them every time we have rainy-day schedule at school and says they're caused by stress."

"Is stress like pneumonia?" Jack asked his brother. "Can we catch it if we've been in the bathroom with her?"

As his sons began a discussion on contagious diseases, Marcus dragged his hand through his short-cropped blondish-brown hair. Violet remembered he'd once worn it much longer, and it used to hold more traces of sun-bleached blond. Now, there were several stubby gray strands near his temples.

"Sorry," he said to her over the boys' heads. "You know how inquisitive kids can be."

His words were probably well-intentioned, but they pierced her heart all the same. Actually, Violet didn't know much about kids at all. She'd grown up an only child, and after everything that had happened when she and Marcus had split up, she'd shied away from interacting with young children when she could avoid it. It was just too painful. She shook her head. "Please don't apologize for them. I think it's sweet that they care so much."

Unlike their father, who hadn't bothered checking on her fourteen years ago when she'd miscarried *their* twins.

"I'd like to say that they usually don't follow strangers into the bathroom and try to diagnose them, but this is the third time. This school year."

"Oh." She blinked several times.

"We didn't follow Mr. Burnworth into the bathroom," Jordan pointed out. "He was standing behind the bakery counter, and his face and mouth were all hard and mean-looking, and I asked him if he needed a tetanus shot because he might have lockjaw."

Violet studied the boy. "You sure know a lot about this kind of stuff for only being… How old are you?"

"We're six and three-quarters," Jordan replied proudly, revealing a missing top tooth.

"That means we're almost seven," Jack explained, holding up the corresponding fingers. "We're gonna have a big birthday party at the ranch, and you can come if you're not contagious."

"That's not for two more months, though," Marcus jumped in. "I'm sure Miss Cortez-Hill will be going back to Dallas way before then."

She jerked up her chin. "How did you know I live in Dallas?"

Marcus shrugged, but not before she caught a flicker of something in his eyes. Guilt, maybe, because he quickly masked it by saying, "I figured it was a safe guess, seeing as how you were never one to stray too far from where your parents wanted you."

The pointed jab was a red herring meant to distract her from the fact that he was trying to downplay something—likely the fact that he'd just overplayed his hand. Some of the best attorneys in Texas had tried the same diversionary tactic in the courtroom with her and failed miserably. She wasn't about to let the guy who broke her heart get away with it. She crossed her arms over her chest. "Or maybe you've been keeping tabs on me, Marcus King."

His eyes rolled a bit too dramatically and she had her answer, even if he tried to deny it. "It's hard not to when our parents have always run in the same political circles. Or at least used to." Marcus glanced away a little too quickly, but not before she saw the shift of emotion pass across his face. He cleared his throat, then added, "Speaking of which, we really need to get going. We're due at the ranch for the graveside service."

"Of course. Please give your mom my condolences and tell her... Wait. The motorcade already left. Shouldn't you have been in one of the family limos?"

"Dad hates limos," Jordan said. "We hadta come in the patrol unit because Dad is always on duty. You want to ride with us?"

"Yeah," Jack added before either of the adults could respond. "You can sit in the front seat and turn on the siren if you want."

Patrol unit? Siren? Violet reassessed Marcus's dark tailored suit, his broad shoulders narrowing down to his waist and the shadow of a bulge directly above his right hip. Her ex-boyfriend was now a cop. And he was currently wearing a gun and holster at his own father's funeral. He'd always been a fun-loving yet responsible guy. But perhaps he was taking his job a little too seriously.

She was about to explain that she hadn't planned to attend the graveside service—which was supposed to only be for family and close friends—but before she could politely decline, Marcus answered on her behalf. "Boys, I'm sure Miss Cortez-Hill has other plans."

She realized this was the third time he'd referred to her as *Miss*. Either he was assuming that she couldn't possibly be married—which was a little insulting—or he knew her marital status the same way he'd known where she was living, which made her wonder what else he knew about her. Suddenly, she didn't feel like allowing him to have the upper hand anymore. Or dictating her plans.

"Actually, I'd love a ride," she told the boys. Then she looked their father directly in the eyes and said, "Thanks for the thoughtful offer."

Marcus steered his county-issued SUV through the gates of the Twin Kings Ranch, nodding at the Secret Service agents stationed at the front entrance. His family's working cattle ranch was over fifty-five thousand acres, and it took almost ten minutes to follow the main road past the house where he'd grown up, and then wind up to the private cemetery plot on a grassy bluff overlooking the Snake River.

His jaw throbbed from the way he'd kept his back molars clamped into place, nearly grinding them together as he tried to ignore the familiar scent of Violet's jasmine perfume. The same one she'd worn when they'd been eighteen. Or maybe his head was just pounding from his sons' incessant chattering the entire ride from the church.

Apparently, Violet's migraine had eased up. She was facing the back seat as much as her seat belt would allow and patiently answering the twins' rapid-fire questions about her favorite ice cream (mint chip—no surprise), her favorite superhero (Wonder Woman—again, no surprise), her dog's name (she didn't have a pet—somewhat of a surprise considering the fact that she'd always loved animals) and if she played any sports (running—very surprising since she'd always hated going for jogs with him when he'd been training for boot camp).

The one question that his children didn't ask was if Violet had any kids. Marcus should've been thankful that his normally inquisitive twins weren't bringing up such a painful subject. After all, he'd tried to put that unfortunate business behind him, even when he'd occasionally hear news about her from his parents or his sister Tessa, who'd interviewed Senator Cortez-Hill several times on her show. But when he'd introduced her to Jack and Jordan, her face had gone completely pale, as though she'd seen a ghost.

It could've been a simple case of her not feeling well, because she'd rushed into the bathroom right after. Yet there had been something else. He could sense it, lurking beneath the tension of their already-uncomfortable reunion. Marcus was suddenly dying to ask her about it. Even if it meant reliving the past.

He backed into the last turnaround spot on the dirt road leading up to the cemetery. It was unseasonably warm for mid-January in Wyoming. Most of the snow from the New Year's storm had already melted, but they'd still have to hike a few hundred yards in the uneven terrain to reach the gravesite.

"I'm sure there would've been room for more vehicles up ahead," Violet said as she tried to navigate around a mud puddle in the middle of their path, her expensive-looking high heel sinking into the damp earth.

"In case of an emergency, though, I need to be able to get my car out quickly."

She made a deliberate show of scanning the dozen or so Secret Service agents surrounding the immediate area, before jerking her chin toward several military personnel dressed in full uniform. "You think you're the only person here who can respond to an emergency situation?"

"I'm the sheriff of Ridgecrest County and responsible for the safety of all the residents and businesses. So my duty extends well beyond this ranch."

"You're also Roper King's son. I'm sure you can take a day off for your father's funeral," Violet said, right before stumbling when her heel caught on a hidden rock.

He quickly grabbed her elbow to steady her, and a current of electricity shot through his hand and up his arm. Marcus nearly released her just as quickly but thought that would suggest he couldn't handle his response to touching her. Instead, he commanded his brain to think of her the same way he'd think of old Mrs. Crenshaw, who held up traffic for at least five minutes every time she slowly crossed Stampede Boulevard, the main street running through town. "Like my son said, I'm always on duty."

She paused to stare at him, and he forgot all about traffic and little old ladies as his pulse picked up speed. To Violet's credit, she didn't pull away from him, either. But he could tell from the rosy-bronze hue spreading along her upper chest and neck that she was equally affected by his touch. It was the same way she used to flush with heat when they were younger and he'd kiss her just above her—

"Why is your skin all reddish like that?" Jack asked Violet before Marcus's inappropriate thoughts could gain any more steam.

"It looks like a rash. Do you have any allergies?" Jordan wanted to know, and Marcus silently cursed himself for allowing his young son to spend so much time researching medical ailments.

Violet cleared her throat, but her blush only intensified. "None that I know of."

Marcus felt his mother's eyes on them and realized the minister was already speaking to the much smaller crowd who'd arrived from the church before them.

He nudged his sons forward toward the two rows of chairs. "There's a couple of empty seats behind

Gan Gan. Why don't you guys go sit down? Quietly," he added. "I'll be right behind you."

Thankfully, Jack and Jordan obeyed, which only happened about 75 percent of the time. Probably because they were too overwhelmed by the sadness of all the adults around them.

The boys sat next to their young cousin and their Aunt Finn, who was great at whispering jokes and keeping the tears at bay during the most solemn of ceremonies.

Marcus didn't want this building tension between him and Violet adding to his sons' distress on an already emotional day, so he didn't immediately follow them. But that left him standing beside Violet during the most emotional and intimate part of the funeral proceedings. Not just beside her but mere inches away since his hand was still on her elbow.

He could hear her soft breathing during the gospel singer's rendition of "Amazing Grace." He could feel the rigidity in her arm during the bugler playing "Taps." He flinched with her during the twenty-one-gun salute. And somehow, he found his own hand intertwined with hers as they lowered his father's casket into the ground. Just as his throat constricted with emotion, Violet lightly squeezed her fingers around his palm, giving him a boost of strength.

Roper King's death had been quite a shock for all of them, but even more so for Marcus, who was still angry at himself for not being more aware. Even though Roper had been bigger than life and damn near invincible, he was also older and they all should've been better prepared for the inevitable. Especially coming only a few years after another loss that had been much more life-altering.

In fact, the family burial plot was the last place he should be holding hands with Violet. Shame immediately washed over him, overshadowing his grief. He quickly untangled his fingers from hers and edged away, unable to keep the gruffness from his voice when he said, "I have to go."

His footsteps were heavy and weighted with guilt when he joined his mother and siblings as they filed into a line to pay their final respects to his father— the man who had taught Marcus how to be a man, how to be a husband and, most importantly, how to be a dad.

Truckloads of flowers had been delivered to both the ranch and the church and were still being silently unloaded behind a cluster of mourners. His immediate family made their way to the cars that would take them back down the hill to the main house and the catered reception his mother had planned for only their closest relatives and friends. However, Marcus grabbed an arrangement of pale pink roses and walked over to a headstone, feeling the weight of his sadness settle deeply onto his shoulders.

Violet stood there awkwardly as the remaining mourners filed past Roper King's open grave. Once, she'd thought of the younger Kings as the siblings she'd never had, but who knew what Marcus had told them after he'd all but abandoned her all those years ago.

Not that any of them would ever be less than cordial to her if she was to approach them. But at that moment, she didn't feel right intruding on their grief just to ease the guilt of attending such an intimate service that was clearly only meant for close family and friends—neither of which she could claim. At least not anymore.

She saw Tessa King walking with a man she didn't recognize but looked to be Secret Service. A second man she *did* recognize—a young up-and-coming congressman from California—approached Marcus's sister, and Violet heard a camera shutter clicking away behind her.

Only preapproved members of the press would be allowed to be here to document the private ceremony, so Violet didn't think anything of it. Instead, she tried to focus on how she was going to get back down the hill and possibly catch a ride to the airport.

There were several men wearing cowboy hats standing around a late-model pickup with the Twin Kings Ranch logo on the door. Roper had been loved by everyone, especially his private employees, so it would make sense for many of the ranch hands to be in attendance. Maybe she could ask one of them for a lift, because she certainly wasn't going to ask Marcus for one.

Her palm was still tingling from where his hand

had clung tightly to hers during the final moments of the service. She'd seen a tear slip beneath the rim of his dark sunglasses, and despite all the heartbreak he'd once caused her, she couldn't make herself walk away from him when he'd seemed to need support most.

Not surprisingly, when everything was said and done, he'd dropped her hand and simply walked away from her. Just like he had all those years ago. Leaving her all by herself, to figure out where to go from here.

Jordan, the twin with the seemingly encyclopedic knowledge about medical conditions, approached Violet cautiously. "Are you still having your migraine? If your blood pressure feels high, you might need to sit down." The boy scrunched his nose at the folding chairs now being loaded into the back of the ranch truck. "Or I can walk you back to the car."

Actually, Violet's head had been the least of her worries this past hour. Her medication had thankfully taken effect before they'd left the church, and she didn't have to force a smile at the sweet boy who seemed to genuinely care about her health. "No, I'm all better. In fact, I was just thinking I feel so great I might walk down to the main house."

Then she could ask someone in the stables to call her a cab.

"But that's, like, fifty miles away," Jack, the other twin, said as he approached with much less caution, narrowly missing tripping over an old wooden head-

stone. "And our aunt says there's only *one* chocolate cake at the house without nuts. I hate nuts, so
we have to get down the hill fast before all the good
desserts are gone."

Most of the cars were already pulling away, and
she finally noticed that it was just her and the twins
left. She looked to her right and left, then asked,
"Where's your dad?"

"He's over there with our mom." Jordan pointed
to a spot behind her, and Violet squeezed her eyes
shut, not wanting to look. Was Marcus still married?
He hadn't been wearing a ring, but some men didn't
wear them. Maybe their mother had ridden here in
a family limo. Maybe she'd been sitting in the second row with the boys the entire time.

Violet slowly turned around, bracing herself for
an awkward introduction. But instead of seeing
Marcus speaking to a woman, she saw him standing under the shady branches of an old sycamore
tree, placing a spray of pale pink roses in front of a
white marble headstone.

Jack slipped his smaller hand in hers, and she was
surprised that her fingers reflexively curled around
his. "Now Grandpa is in Heaven with Mommy."

Chapter Three

Marcus was seriously looking forward to grabbing a bottle of sixteen-year-old single barrel bourbon and heading straight into his own wing of the house to zone out in front of the television with the boys as they rewatched one of their favorite movies. It had been a hell of an afternoon and they all needed a comforting, yet familiar distraction. But first he needed to figure out what to do with his ex-girlfriend.

After a silent ride down the hill from the cemetery, the boys eagerly ran inside the main house to join their Uncle Duke, who'd been waiting for them on the porch. His brother must've seen them together before leaving the cemetery and known Marcus would need a few moments. Now it was just him and Violet standing in front of his SUV in the wide parking area near the steps of the kitchen porch.

"Uh...do you want to come inside?" he asked against his better judgment. After all, his mother would give him hell if she knew that Violet was here and he didn't at least extend an invite.

"I really shouldn't," she said. "In fact, I already missed my flight back to Dallas and should get to Jackson Hole soon if I'm going to try and get another connection tonight."

He nodded, equally disappointed—and oddly relieved.

"Listen," she started, then tilted her head and paused. As though she was thinking better of whatever she'd been about to say. He lowered his chin and was about to encourage her to keep going when her soft lips parted. "I'm sorry about your wife. I saw you," she explained when he blinked several times, clearly startled. "You were placing flowers on a grave, and one of the twins told me—Jack, I think. I know it's none of my business, but how did she pass away?"

"He told you?" Marcus experienced the sour taste of dread every time someone mentioned his wife. Part of the reason he hated funerals so much was because it not only reminded him of what he and his sons had lost but how everyone had treated them afterward. Marcus hated reliving all the pitying looks and tut-tuts about how tragic it was for him to be a widower so young and for the boys to be without their mother. While he wanted to appreciate their well-meaning sympathy, all it did was reinforce his own doubts about his ability to be a single father. Over the years, though, he'd found the best way of dealing with questions about Brie's death was to be as matter-of-fact about it as possible.

"She had a brain aneurysm. The twins were only eighteen months old, and yeah, it was quite a shock. One of those freak things that nobody can explain. I think that's why Jordan is so obsessed with medicine. He's naturally curious and started reading at a young age. He had all these questions about his mom and why she died, and I guess none of our explanations made sense to him. So he started looking for his own answers."

"Your sons are very caring and kind and thought… thoughtful." Her voice quivered, and she drew in a deep breath before she continued. "You're very lucky to have them."

"That's what everyone told me after Brie died." He lifted his face to the afternoon sky, the sun starting to make its way closer to the Teton mountain range. "How lucky I was to still have a piece of her."

"No, I meant you're lucky to have them, period. Even if your wife was still here, I would tell you the same thing. Your children are a blessing. You're a very fortunate man, Marcus. Not everyone will get to have that same experience, let alone twice."

His heartbeat stopped before picking up speed.

"Back at the church, right before you uh…threw up… you seemed really surprised that I had twins."

She tilted her head and narrowed her eyes at him, as though the answer should have been obvious to him. "Because *we* were supposed to have twins. There were two babies when I miscarried."

Marcus's knees buckled, and his hand propped against the hood of the SUV was the only thing that kept him from going down.

"You…*miscarried*?" His voice was much louder than he'd expected, and one of the caterers carrying a stainless-steel tray from their van looked across the driveway at them.

"Of course I miscarried." Violet blinked several times, her black spiky lashes like tiny daggers to his heart. "Wait. You didn't think I…that I had an abortion?"

Marcus scrubbed a hand over his face in frustration. "I didn't know what to think because I never heard from you. All I knew was that you took the pregnancy test right before I left for boot camp, and then nothing else. At my graduation, I asked my parents if they'd heard from you, and my dad said your mom had gone out of her way to talk to him on Capitol Hill. She wanted to pass along a message that you'd made a *tough choice*—" he used his fingers for air quotes "—but were so glad you did because you were loving college life and could finally focus on your future. At first, I was so pissed, and then the betrayal set in. Not at your decision, but at the fact that you couldn't even bother to tell me yourself."

Her tone grew steely. "I *did* make a tough choice, Marcus. I *chose* to have your babies. But in the end, the decision was out of my hands. Either way, how could you think that I wouldn't have told you what happened?"

Confusion snaked through him, making everything go blurry, and he shook his head to clear his thoughts. All these years, he'd assumed Violet had changed her mind about him and the future they'd discussed. He'd believed she'd moved on with her life, and even though he'd been hurt, he hadn't judged her. They'd only been eighteen, after all. "Then why didn't I know?"

"I knew they'd taken away your phone in boot camp. It wasn't like I could call you and talk about it. The best I could do was send you a letter right after it happened."

A letter? He began pacing as he absorbed her words. He'd gotten only a few letters from his parents, but none from anyone else. Not even his friends back home.

His hands flew up in the air in frustration before clasping on top of his head as he stretched out the tension exploding in his shoulders. "I never got it. I swear, Violet, if I had known you'd miscarried, I would've gone AWOL to be by your side."

Suddenly, his frustration turned to a sharp anger. How could she have thought so little of him? He was about to ask her exactly that when his youngest brother came slamming out of the kitchen door.

"Hey, Violet, what are you doing here?" Mitchell Junior, better known as MJ to his older siblings, was the baby of the family. "I haven't seen you since that time you and Marcus took me to the Spring Fling Festival, and you guys made me sit by myself on the Ferris wheel so you could make out."

"I don't remember that," Marcus snapped, annoyed at his little brother's interruption of their emotionally charged conversation.

"Unfortunately, I *do* remember that." Violet's frown made it look as though she was cringing. "That was pretty selfish of us. Didn't you end up puking halfway through the ride, and the operator made us hose out the car where you were sitting?"

Now, *that* part Marcus remembered. Violet had taken MJ to the bathroom to clean him up, and Marcus had been left with a traveling carny named Smoke or Blade or some other nefarious moniker who took a cigarette break as Marcus fought an old garden hose to scrub out his kid brother's mess. It was what he'd deserved for not taking better care of his younger brother.

"Where are you going?" Marcus asked his brother.

"Aunt Freckles doesn't like Mom's soy butter, so she gave me some money to go to the store and get some special brand. She said to sneak out of here before Uncle Rider finds out where I'm going and asks me to get him a can of dip."

Uncle Rider, their dad's twin brother, was a tough-as-nails eighty-year-old cowboy struggling to follow his doctor's advice to quit chewing tobacco. Aunt Freckles, Rider's estranged wife, loved cooking for her extended family almost as much as she loved driving her former husband crazy.

It wasn't until the kid drove away that Marcus remembered the market in town had been closed today for the funeral. The only businesses that had stayed open were the gas station and the liquor store.

That should've been Marcus's first clue that things were only going to get worse from here.

Violet was still reeling from the revelation that Marcus hadn't known she'd miscarried.

She was even more upset that he'd spent all these years assuming she hadn't wanted their children. So much hurt and heartache could have been cleared up if only they'd been able to talk to each other all those years ago. She'd been about to say as much when his younger brother had come outside and interrupted their heated conversation.

Which was probably for the best. Clearly, the day of his father's funeral wasn't the best time or place to argue about the secret they'd hidden from his family or to angrily rehash all their old mistakes. She looked at her watch. Damn. She should've asked MJ for a ride into town. No way was she going to make the last flight out at this rate.

The kitchen door opened, and Jordan poked his

head outside and looked directly at Violet. "Are you getting another migraine?"

"Who has a migraine?" a woman asked. Violet would have recognized that voice anywhere.

Sherilee King.

Marcus's mom had been the quintessential politician's wife. A woman with impeccable manners and no tolerance for anyone who didn't have her family's best interest at heart. Despite her closeness with the rest of the King family all those years ago, Violet had never been able to tell if Sherilee liked her or hated her—probably a little of both—and always wondered if Marcus's mother had somehow influenced his decision to not contact Violet after the miscarriage. Obviously, she didn't have to wonder about the second part any longer. According to Marcus, it was her own mother who'd caused the damage. Still. The protective matriarch of the King family was a force to be reckoned with.

Growing up the daughter of the powerful and vocal Senator Cortez-Hill, Violet was well-accustomed to female role models with strong opinions. But Sherilee King was one of the few women who Violet considered downright intimidating. Or at least she used to feel that way when she'd been a teenager and had binge-watched all *The Godfather* movies with her father. Marcus's mom had the uncanny ability to give off a serious mafia boss–type of vibe while looking like an upscale suburban housewife. Like she could order fancy designer cupcakes for the women's-club luncheon just as easily as she could order a hit on someone for daring to wear sneakers under their gown to one of her black-tie galas.

When the older woman stepped around her grandson and out onto the porch, Violet managed a weak smile and a wave.

"Hi, Mrs. King." Violet didn't dare address her by her first name. "I'm very sorry for your loss. Mr. King was always so kind to me whenever we saw each other, and I'll always have fond memories of him."

Sherilee's face softened into a brief smile, but then her professionally styled hair stayed in place as her head moved right to left, scanning the long driveway and parking area the size of a strip mall. "Your mother isn't here, is she?"

"No, ma'am." Violet shook her head quickly, her own uncombed hair falling into her face. It was no secret that Sherilee King and Eva Cortez-Hill were friendly with each other when the media was present, but when the cameras were gone, they were like a pair of rival gang leaders waiting for the other to throw the first verbal punch. "My parents left after the church service. I was just about to call for an Uber or a cab so I could catch a later flight."

"Don't be ridiculous," Sherilee said, causing Violet to immediately feel ridiculous. The woman put an arm around her grandson, lovingly pulling the concerned boy against the side of her tailored black pencil skirt. "And don't be so formal. One of Marcus's deputies or our stable foreman can give you a ride to the airport. Unless you have your dad's private jet on standby, you might be hard-pressed to find an open seat on a commercial flight. But if you have a migraine, you should come into the house and lie down. Marcus, go get Violet a glass of wine or something stronger to take the edge off."

Jordan lifted his serious face to his grandmother's. "Actually, Gan Gan, alcohol wouldn't be very good for Miss Violet if she has a migraine."

"What about a soda?" Sherilee consulted the young child as though he was wearing a white lab coat and had an advanced medical degree. "The caffeine might help?"

"You know, my headache is long gone," Violet said before Marcus's mom and son could finish their unsolicited medical assessment. "Truly, I'm fine and don't want to impose any more than I already have—"

"Dear," Sherilee said as she put up a palm, her enormous diamond ring flashing in the afternoon sun as she interrupted, "it's been a rough day for all of us, okay? Now, Jordan here is worried about your health, and he's going to keep coming outside to check on you until he's convinced you're better. You've always been a good girl, despite having a hardheaded shark for a mother. You don't want to worry the boys needlessly, do you?"

Violet's mouth was hanging open as she tried to

figure out if she'd just been praised or chastised. Likely both.

"Marcus, why are you still standing there?" Sherilee asked. "I said bring Violet inside."

"Mom, please. She's a grown woman." Marcus crossed his arms over his chest. "I'm not going to throw her over my shoulder and carry her through the door if she doesn't want to go."

"Do you see what I have to put up with, Violet dear?" Sherilee rubbed her smooth forehead, which was reputed to have been surgically enhanced by some of the top cosmetic surgeons in the world. "The older my kids get, the more rebellious they are."

That was twice Sherilee King had called her *dear*, making Violet much more tempted to accept the offer of a cold drink and maybe even the piece of chocolate cake without walnuts Jack had mentioned earlier—if any was left. Plus, drowsiness was one of the side effects from the medication she'd taken earlier and was just now starting to kick in. She could use some caffeine, come to think of it...

"You think *I'm* rebellious?" Marcus asked his mom, who flicked her wrist dismissively at him. Clearly, this was an old argument she didn't have the patience to hear again. Yet, her son was determined to continue as though he was itching for a fight with someone and anyone would do. "What about Finn and Dahlia? What about MJ? Did you know he just—"

"Stop," Violet whispered, cutting Marcus off mid-sentence. "If you start listing all of the transgressions your siblings ever committed, we'll be here all night. Besides, your mom's right. It's been a long day for everyone. I'll come inside for a bit and get something to eat and drink, and then I'll be on my way."

He threw his hands in the air and shrugged. "Fine. But I have every intention of finishing our earlier conversation."

An hour later, Violet had been heartily welcomed into the bosom of the King inner circle as though she hadn't been gone for fourteen years. All three of Marcus's sisters—Tessa, Dahlia and Finn—hugged Violet the moment they saw her.

His brother Duke, still wearing his Navy dress uniform, lifted her off her feet and spun her around. When he set her on her feet, he whispered, "I was waiting for Marcus to get over the shock of seeing you again before coming over and saying hi. Thanks for coming. It means a lot to have you here."

Duke was only a year younger and, as far as she knew, had been the only King who'd known about her pregnancy. It was likely he'd also assumed the worst about her just as Marcus had. So it gave her a boost of confidence to know that he was glad to see her.

Duke introduced her to his handsome and charming husband, Tom, who was a surgeon in the Navy. After Jordan's insistent prompting, Tom asked Violet a few routine questions before assuring his young nephew. "It is my professional opinion that the patient is not suffering any long-lasting effects of her earlier migraine."

"I think someone should go tell Dad," Jack said. "He keeps staring over here at Miss Violet and frowning."

Duke chuckled. "Don't worry about your dad, kid-dos. He's probably just grumpy all the brownies are gone already. Why don't you go see if the caterers put out any more?"

Marcus's boys finally went off to the dessert table with their cousin Amelia, and Violet was surprised to realize she was actually way more comfortable than she'd expected to be. Surrounded once again by the family she'd loved so much, she finally began to relax. There was no way he would bring up the subject of her miscarriage or their breakup with so many witnesses.

The main house at the Twin Kings was nearly twelve thousand square feet, and there were still plenty of friends and neighbors in attendance at the reception following the funeral. She ate a little food, said hello to a few of the people she already knew and then found an unoccupied sitting area in the corner where she could escape from the curious glances and scroll through her phone as she tried to hold back several yawns. As long as Violet pretended to ignore his stormy stares from across the hotel lobby–sized living room, she was able to avoid Marcus—for the most part.

Thank God he had his back to her when he took

off his suit jacket and rolled up his shirtsleeves, because it was the one time she hadn't been able to look away. His shoulders rolled back in circles as he stretched, and her palms suddenly itched to feel the tense muscles underneath and slowly massage away the day's stress.

Instead, she chugged her watered down iced tea in an effort to make her mouth less dry and her cheeks less warm. She needed to get out of here before she lost complete control.

Eventually, Violet was able to catch the attention of a Secret Service agent who was going off duty, and she snuck out of the Kings' house through the busy kitchen without so much as a goodbye.

It was better this way, she thought, as she rode in the back seat of one of the catering vans that was returning to Jackson Hole. No awkward goodbyes, no promises to keep in touch when everyone knew they wouldn't.

Plus, she wanted to talk to her mother in person and ask her if she'd really implied that Violet had had an abortion. Not that she didn't believe Marcus, but she wanted to find out why on earth her mom had done such a thing.

Oh, who was she kidding? The woman would argue that she'd been trying to protect Violet. And the truth was that her mom had been the one to physically take care of her when she'd slid into a postpartum depression afterward.

But confronting anyone would have to wait another day.

Sherilee King had been right when she'd warned that most of the commercial flights out of town were full. Even most of the hotels were packed with avid skiers who'd booked their vacations in advance, as well as guests who'd come to pay tribute to the former vice president. Violet was lucky to get a room at a nondescript chain motel and hoped she'd be able to rent a car the next day and drive to an airport in a bigger city.

Even though the medication she'd taken earlier had wiped out the worst of the headache, it had left her a little groggy, especially after the events of the day. It also helped her fall asleep the moment her head hit the pillow. When her cell phone rang early the following morning, Violet struggled to open her eyes and tapped the green button before her brain had the chance to wonder who was calling her from a Washington, DC, area code.

"Violet! You haven't left town yet, have you?"

"Mrs. King?" Violet squinted at the bedside clock that read 7:03 a.m. "What's wrong?"

"I need a criminal defense attorney."

Technically, Violet was a public defender, which meant she wasn't for hire. But if Sherilee King had the resources to track her down, then the woman already knew that fact and wasn't about to let a little thing like retainer fees or state bar requirements stop her. Violet sat up in bed and asked, "For yourself?"

"No, not for myself." The woman muttered a curse. "For MJ. Marcus went and arrested his own brother last night. How soon can you get down to the Ridgecrest County Courthouse?"

"I know what you're trying to do, Mom, and it won't work," Marcus said as he followed his mother up the wide back-porch steps of the main house on the family's ranch later that morning. "Hiring Violet to represent MJ is *not* going to make me drop the charges."

"I'm trying to save my youngest son from being framed for a crime he didn't commit," Sheri-lee snapped back at him before stomping into the kitchen. "You know what would happen to a young, impressionable kid like MJ in prison."

"MJ is *not* going to prison," Marcus practically growled in frustration. "He was charged with underage drinking and resisting arrest. It's a misdemeanor."

His mom's professionally shaped eyebrows lifted. "If it's no big deal, then why are you still holding him in a jail cell?"

"I didn't say it wasn't a big deal. MJ went out drinking with Deputy Broman's eighteen-year-old daughter last night. When her dad busted them, MJ punched the man—a sworn peace officer on duty."

"So says Deputy Broman." His mother pointed a manicured finger at Marcus's chest. "You know that guy has it in for our family. How do you know he isn't making this up to make you look bad before next year's election?"

"Besides the fact that Broman has a black eye and MJ had a blood alcohol level of twice the legal limit? My deputies wear body cameras, and I saw the video footage."

"Damn it!" His mom picked up one of Aunt Freckles's famous homemade biscuits, slathered it with honey butter and then loaded it down with a couple of cold pieces of leftover bacon before shoving half of it in her mouth. So much for her claimed vegan lifestyle. Sherilee King only ate like this when she was under extreme stress. Her lipstick was still covered in crumbs when she asked, "Okay, so how about we compromise. You give MJ a warning or a ticket or something and release him to my custody?"

"As if that'll teach the kid a lesson." Marcus snorted. "Listen, Mom, I know you don't want to hear this, but MJ has been flying under the radar and getting away with stuff us older kids never would have gotten past you and Dad. Do you have any idea how blatantly biased it would be for the county sheriff to turn a blind eye to illegal behavior just because it's his kid brother doing it? If we don't make him face the music now, his next arrest could possibly be a felony. Is that what you want?"

"What I *want* is for my kids to look out for each other. To protect each other."

Marcus refused to cave. "Well, this is my way of looking out for him. Consider it an intervention."

Marcus suddenly realized that none of his adult siblings were stepping foot in the kitchen right now. What did they know that he didn't?

"And that's why I hired Violet to represent him." His mom put her hands on her hips, and he saw a quick flash of a knowing smirk, a determined glint in her eye. "Because maybe you need an intervention of your own."

A cold shiver raced down the back of Marcus's neck. "What's that supposed to mean?"

"You were in the briefing room with the Secret Service agents just a few minutes ago." His mother jerked her head toward the custom-built bunkhouse across the main road. The one that housed their father's assigned security detail whenever he'd traveled from Washington to visit the family home. "This has the potential to become a really big deal, and you can't be on duty all the time. You can't designate yourself the family protector when there is too much other stuff going on. If it wasn't tough enough dealing with your father's death and funeral, now we've got the media scandal of the year with Tessa fainting in that agent's arms yesterday. It's only a matter of time before all those reporters lined up outside the gate find out about MJ, too." Her tone softened. "Look, Marcus, I get it that you want to teach him a lesson, and I'm sure you're right. But now's really not the best time to do it."

Marcus rolled his eyes. "Then maybe MJ should have picked a more convenient time to polish off a liter of vodka before trying to make it to second base with Deputy Broman's daughter."

"Allegedly," someone said in the doorway behind Marcus. He turned to find Violet following his aunt Freckles into the kitchen, and his adrenaline spiked at the sight of his ex-girlfriend.

Her jet-black hair was in a high ponytail on top of her head, and her beautiful face didn't have a trace of makeup, causing her to appear just as young and carefree as she had been all those years ago when they'd naively thought they'd be together forever. However, her professional tone and the adversarial squaring of her shoulders reminded him that she was all grown up now and clearly ready to go to battle against him.

"Excuse me?" he asked, realizing too late that he should have kept his mouth shut.

"My client *allegedly* drank vodka with Deputy Broman's daughter. Although, he might be willing to stipulate to the circumstances surrounding the second-base allegation, since it will prove that the arresting officer had questionable motives for making the arrest in the first place."

So that's how she wanted to play this. Marcus drew in a deep breath, trying to ignore the unexpected sting of betrayal. Unfortunately, he opened his mouth once again before his emotions were completely under control. "I'm not shocked that an attorney would twist the facts to their advantage. What's shocking is that my mom got you to agree to this."

"You can call it twisting the facts." Violet lifted one shoulder in a shrug, and he noticed she was wearing the same clothes she'd had on yesterday. "I call it a fair trial, something everyone is entitled to under the United States Constitution. There's this little part in there called the Sixth Amendment, which guarantees all defendants a right to an attorney. Even when those defendants are little brothers who piss you off."

Marcus felt his nostrils flare as he expelled a frustrated breath. "I never said MJ doesn't have a right to a fair trial. Or to a lawyer. I just don't see why it has to be *you.*"

"Because if *you* were arrested, Marcus, you would want the best representing you."

"The best?" Marcus knew she'd always been wickedly smart, but when had she become so presumptuous? Or so full of herself? The Violet he'd once known had been sweet and humble and slightly shy. In fact, she'd been scared to death to tell their parents after they'd sat staring at that positive pregnancy-test stick for what had seemed like days. However, now she was anything but shy—proudly facing off against him in the heart of the King domain, looking like she was ready to start her cross-examination. And apparently he'd somehow managed to land himself in her witness stand.

She gently clasped her hands in front of her, a tactic he knew was meant to seem disarming, and asked, "You mean to tell me that when you were keeping tabs on me all these years, you never came across my acquittal record at trial?"

"I wasn't keeping tabs," Marcus defended himself. He knew he'd slipped yesterday when he'd made a reference to her living in Dallas and introduced her to the boys as *Miss* Cortez-Hill. But it wasn't like he'd actively searched for information about her. "It just so happens that I follow a lot of baseball commentators online, including your dad. It's not my fault that he posts about you a lot on his social-media page."

"Oh, I heard about people doing that online-stalking thing." Aunt Freckles's eyes widened knowingly, which caused her unusually long false lashes to flicker against the brightness of her heavy green eye shadow. "They get these fake accounts so they can secretly follow people and snoop around in their business. I think the kids call it catfishing."

"I think you mean creeping." Marcus cringed as he shook his head. "But I wasn't doing that. Or catfishing, or anything else so desperate."

"No one said you were, darlin'." His aunt tutted through her bright magenta lipstick, then adjusted the cropped lime-green sweater that didn't quite meet the waistband of her jungle-print yoga pants. The woman had to be pushing eighty, yet had a tendency to dress in tight, revealing clothes that would make most eighteen-year-olds blush. "I was just pointing out to Violet that us single gals always have to be on the lookout for men with bad intentions."

"Oh, no, Aunt Freckles!" Violet turned to his aunt before Marcus could further defend himself or his intentions. "I didn't realize you were single now. I thought for sure you and Uncle Rider were going to get back together."

"Why do you care?" Marcus asked, not bothering to hide the annoyance lacing his voice. Of all the things he and Violet should be discussing, this was a topic that could wait a bit longer. "Are you a divorce attorney now, too? Maybe my family can get some sort of group rate."

"Nobody has time for your snide comments right now, Marcus." His mother reached for another biscuit and the butter knife. "Violet needs to go to her room and change so we can get to the courthouse in time for the bail hearing this afternoon. We need to make a strong defensive case right out of the gate so I can get my baby home where he belongs."

"It's more of a formality than a hearing," he corrected, trying to ignore the muscle ticking beside his eye. In fact, once Judge Calhoun sets the bail amount, Marcus had planned to post the bond himself. That way, MJ would be released to Marcus's custody, and then he could drive the boy home and have a heart-to-heart talk with him. "Besides, I thought you wanted to keep the arrest out of the media. Having Violet there would only draw more attention to... Wait. Did you just say she was going to *her room* to change?"

"Well, I certainly can't change here in the kitchen,"

Violet replied, placing her hand over the wide V of her exposed neckline. Marcus's eyes drew to the soft, tanned skin there before immediately pushing away the sudden inappropriate thought of her taking off that rumpled black dress.

"I meant a room *here*." Marcus's muscles flexed instinctively. "At *this* house?"

"You know there isn't a suitable hotel in Teton Ridge," his mother said, her slight smirk flickering again. "Naturally, Violet is going to be staying with us at the Twin Kings."

Freckles clapped her hands together before reaching for an apron. "It'll be just like old times."

"Yeah, except you're all forgetting that things didn't end so well back then." Marcus heard his mother's angry gasp, as well as a tsk from Freckles. Yet his boots echoed his own annoyance with each angry step across the polished wood floors as he stomped to the door, determined to get as far away from this potential disaster as he could. "And that was back when we were at least on the same team."

When he yanked down on the handle to make his escape, his sister, brother and uncle—who'd apparently been pressed against the other side of the door listening—tumbled into the kitchen together.

Marcus muttered a curse, then strode to his SUV without so much as a goodbye.

It looked like he and the twins would temporarily be moving into their old cabin on the ranch. Because there was no way he was staying under the same roof as his ex-girlfriend.

His life was complicated enough as it was.

Chapter Four

Violet spent the morning filing paperwork with the Wyoming Bar Association to allow for pro hac vice status so she could temporarily practice law in the state. Since she was licensed in Texas, Roper's trust and estates attorney in Cheyenne had agreed to act as her local cocounsel, which really just meant that he was vouching for Violet while not coming to Teton Ridge himself.

Then she texted one of her coworkers who lived in the same condo complex back home, asking her to ship some of Violet's professional attire to the Twin Kings Ranch so that she wouldn't have to continue borrowing Sherilee King's couture designer suits. Although wearing Chanel to the county courthouse might not cause as much scandal as the cheetah-print sequined tube top Freckles had lovingly loaned her this morning.

In between all the busy work, Violet had also spent a significant amount of time wondering why she was even going through all this trouble when it was so clear that Marcus didn't want her there. Not that she cared what Marcus wanted. She wasn't doing this for him.

And yet, the more he opposed her presence, the more Violet was determined to stay. So what did that say about her? That she was spoiling for a fight, as well?

Maybe. Maybe, after all these years without answers, she was.

Clearly, though, she wasn't the only one with a chip on her shoulder. There was no way Marcus would've responded with such hostility if his mother had hired any other defense attorney. So then, why was he so angry that it was Violet who'd be doing their family this favor?

Probably because he was harboring some other sort of resentment toward her. The old Violet would have wanted to talk to him, to get to the root of the matter and try to resolve whatever issues were coming between them. But the new Violet had spent the last fourteen years fighting to make herself heard, and she was no longer in the mood to listen. At least not to Marcus, who'd never bothered to contact her after he got out of boot camp to hear what she had to say.

So now that she was standing behind the defense table inside one of the few courtrooms at the Ridgecrest County Courthouse, Violet was even more annoyed to see her ex-boyfriend on the opposite side of the aisle.

"Your Honor," Violet faced the older, gray-haired judge sitting on the bench, "my client is a young man with a promising future and long-standing ties to the community. In fact, he lives in the same house as the sheriff seated behind the prosecutor. Their property is currently under the protection and surveillance of several federal agents, who have been assigned to trail the defendant wherever he goes. Mitchell King Jr. is neither a flight risk nor a danger to the community at large and should be granted bail while he is pending trial."

"Miss Cortez-Hill," the judge said patiently, "the court is well aware of who the defendant is related to and where he lives. In fact, one judge already had to recuse herself from this case because she was the team mom for the defendant's Little League team ten years ago. So unless the parties are going to file a motion for a change of venue, I'm going to allow bail, as is standard for similar charges. But I'm also going to add a gag order restricting all parties from speaking about the case to the media or anyone else outside of this courtroom. I'm not going to have this esteemed institution turn into a full-blown circus just because of the defendant's famous family name. If there's nothing else pending, court is recessed for the day."

Judge Calhoun left the bench, his high-top sneakers under his robe suggesting that he was on his way to the rec center to play pickup basketball. At least, that's what she'd gathered from her earlier meeting with the prosecutor who'd purposely let it slip that he played in the same senior league with the judge and they often traveled to tournaments together.

This was a small town, and she was the outsider.

MJ, who had been allowed to change into the clean clothes his mother had brought him, sagged back into his wooden seat as he rubbed the dark shadows under his eyes. "Does this mean I get to go home?"

"Yes." Violet nodded at him and then leaned closer as she lowered her voice. "But as long as I'm your attorney, you are going to be *staying* at home and staying out of trouble. No more drinking, and no more dates with that deputy's daughter. In fact, consider yourself on quasi–house arrest."

MJ jutted his chin across the courtroom at Marcus. "Is that what big brother told you to tell me?"

"No. That's what *I'm* telling you. If I'm going to represent you and put my professional reputation on the line, then you're going to act like the model citizen that I know your father raised you to be."

At the mention of the late Roper King, his tall eighteen-year-old son slouched sheepishly in his chair. But then something sparkled behind his tired eyes. "Is it true that Marcus didn't want our mom to hire you?"

Violet could deny it, but it was important to establish honesty in an attorney–client relationship. If she wanted MJ to be honest with her, then she needed to be truthful with him. Besides, she was staying at the family ranch, and he was a smart kid. He'd figure it out for himself soon enough. "That's correct."

"Fine. I'll do whatever you say as long as it pisses him off."

"Whatever is going on between you and your brother is between the two of you." Violet stacked a file onto her notepad, making a mental note to have her friend send her briefcase, as well. "I'm not going to tell you that you need to get along. But I will strongly warn you that it is not in your best interest to purposely antagonize the man who eats lunch with the district attorney at Biscuit Betty's every Wednesday."

"You've been in town less than twenty-four hours, and you already know my schedule?" Marcus asked as he casually planted a hip on the defense table.

Refusing to let him tower over her from his perch, she stood and collected the leather tote bag she'd borrowed this morning from Tessa. But standing only brought their faces closer together. She gulped before squaring her shoulders. "I make it my business to know everything I can about my opponents."

"Really, Violet? Opponents? You make it sound

like we're enemies when, at the end of the day, we both want what's best for MJ."

Now MJ rose to his feet. The teen was taller than Marcus by a couple of inches, but the gangliness of youth was still present in his thinner frame. "What's best for me is that you stop treating me like a little kid."

"Yeah, well, this is what happens to grown-ups when they break the law, MJ." Marcus stayed comfortably seated, suggesting to his younger brother that he wasn't the least bit threatened by his height or his irritation. "They go to grown-up court and face grown-up consequences. Welcome to adulthood."

Out of the corner of her eye, Violet saw MJ's fist clenching, and she immediately put a calming hand on his tense arm. "MJ, will you please go check on your mother? Someone needs to intercept her before she tries to follow Judge Calhoun out to his car. Let me handle your brother."

Sherilee King had never met someone who didn't soon owe her a favor, and small towns like this were already ripe for issues of alleged impropriety since everyone knew everyone. The last thing she wanted was a hint of any additional scandal. If Violet was going to win a case, she was going to do so on the merits of the case and her arguments—not on any accusations that outside influences swayed the judge.

MJ gave a tense nod before going after his mother, leaving Violet alone with Marcus.

"And how exactly do you plan on *handling* me,

counselor?" He crossed his arms across his chest, the bulge of his biceps pushing against the fabric of his tan county-issued shirt. Why did he have to look so damn good in his uniform?

"It's a figure of speech, Sheriff. Don't make it awkward." She slung the leather straps of her borrowed tote over her shoulder and started walking toward the exit.

She wasn't surprised to find Marcus on her heels, holding one of the narrow courtroom doors open for her, as he replied, "Then don't make this into some sort of battle where one of us has to lose."

"This battle between you and MJ was obviously brewing well before I got here." She held her breath as she squeezed past him, knowing she'd be a goner if any part of her body so much as grazed against his. "So unless you're following me to offer a sweet deal on behalf of the prosecutor, someone is going to eventually lose. I assure you that it won't be me."

"You may have one of the highest acquittal rates over in Dallas, but even the best criminal defense attorneys can't win them all." He must've seen the shock on her face when he caught up to her because he added, "You're not the only one who knows how to research your so-called opponent."

The fluttering sensation in her stomach was probably due to her missing lunch and not the way his eyes drank her in as he admitted that he'd also spent some time this morning researching her. Or at least her court record.

Luckily, the cool mountain air snapped her back to reality as she stepped outside the courthouse. "At least you can admit that we're on opposing sides. Just remember that it's your brother at the center of this fight, Marcus. Not me. When all of this is over, I'll be back in Dallas with another acquittal under my belt, and you'll still be here in Wyoming dealing with the fallout of your already strained family relationships."

Marcus made an unconvincing harrumph sound. "Unlike some people I know, I've never been afraid of challenging my family members. Tell me, Violet, does your mother know you're staying in Teton Ridge for the foreseeable future?"

"Look, I know that my mom wasn't always welcoming to you when we were younger."

"She led me to believe you had an abortion, Violet. That's how badly she wanted to get me out of your life."

"Trust me, I have that on my list of things to discuss with her. I will do that in my own time and in my own way." She narrowed her eyes. "Is this the road you want to go down, Marcus? Because as soon as you challenge someone, they're bound to challenge you back. Then you'll have to explain why it was so easy for you to believe her and walk away."

"You think I—"

"Violet!" One of the twins yelled from the sidewalk at the bottom of the concrete stairs. It was Jack, because he shook free of Dahlia's hand and accidentally stepped on Sherilee's foot as he rushed by his grandmother to sprint up the steps. Jordan was the rule follower and stayed safely at his aunt's side, licking a vanilla ice cream cone while sending Violet a happy wave.

Jack had what looked to be melted chocolate ice cream around his mouth, and Violet tried not to wince as he hurtled into her with a tight hug. Should she hug him back? It wasn't that she was opposed to physical displays of affection or to chocolate stains. But this was a borrowed suit, and she hadn't seen a dry cleaner on Stampede Boulevard.

When Jack looked up at her, he smiled his gap-toothed grin. "I thought you left yesterday without saying goodbye to us."

At that, she did hug him back, rather awkwardly with a pat on his head. She was equally touched by his words, yet slightly confused. The poor child had been growing up without a mother, and he'd recently lost his grandfather. Of course he would have some separation-anxiety issues, although Violet would never have anticipated he'd react so strongly to a random woman he'd just met yesterday. Still, he deserved to be comforted.

"I'm so sorry, sweetie. I was in a hurry to catch my ride and shouldn't have been so thoughtless. Will you forgive me?"

"Okay," the boy said simply. "Can I sit next to you at dinner tonight?"

Violet glanced at her watch. To her surprise, it was nearly four in the afternoon.

"Here you go, Jack." Marcus pulled a clean napkin out of his back pocket and casually handed it to the boy. Clearly, he kept a supply of them on hand for this exact purpose. "I don't think we're going to have dinner at the main house tonight."

"But we always have a fancy sit-down dinner when Gan Gan is in town."

Marcus's sigh reverberated in his throat. "I know. But with Aunt Tessa and Aunt Freckles and now Miss Cortez-Hill staying there, it's kind of a lot of people."

As though hearing her grandson invoke her name, Sherilee limped up the few stairs separating them, pretending she didn't have a dusty sneaker print covering the expensive Italian leather toe of her high heel. "Don't be ridiculous, Marcus. Of course you and the boys will still be having dinner with—" she paused just long enough to give Violet a pointed look that brooked no argument "—*all of us* at the main house."

"Yes!" Jack pumped a fist in the air before yelling back to his twin. "Hey, Jordan, Violet is gonna sit by us at dinner."

At least someone was happy about it, she thought, trying not to let the excited boys see an ounce of apprehension on her face. Now she would have to endure another round of dysfunctional family dynamics with the Kings.

* * *

"You apologized to my son earlier today," Marcus said to Violet later that evening as they were having predinner cocktails in the great room of the main house. He took another drink from his bottle of craft ale, his second of the night.

Violet's hair was out of that ridiculous tight bun and hung softly down her back. She shoved a loose strand behind her ear, and despite the taste of beer still fresh on his tongue, his mouth went dry. All too swiftly, he recalled the silky feel of her hair in his hands as he… *Ahem. She's speaking, idiot.* "Of course I did. It was rude of me to leave last night without saying goodbye."

"It's weird, though. Usually he has a short attention span when it comes to new people." In fact, neither of his sons had mentioned Violet yesterday after she'd left, and Marcus had assumed they'd easily forgotten about her until his sister Dahlia had dropped them off at the courthouse after school. But saying as much would be admitting that he didn't have a good read on his own children. Because clearly, they did remember Violet, especially Jordan, who'd spent the last fifteen minutes quizzing her on the side effects of her migraine medication. Instead Marcus clarified what he meant. "Adults normally don't go to great lengths to apologize for something kids are likely to forget anyway."

"No? Well, they should."

He'd noticed that she was somewhat stiff when

Jack had hugged her earlier on the courthouse steps. Even now she looked as though she would rather be wearing anything other than the painted macaroni necklace that Jordan had made at school today. His son had ceremoniously given it to her just before joining his brother in the dining room to make sure the place cards their cousin had drawn were still in the right spots. "Do you spend much time around children?"

"I'm an only child, remember?" Violet looked away quickly, refusing to meet his eyes. "No nieces or nephews or big family gatherings like this."

"Yeah, but surely you have friends with kids?"

Her knuckles were white as she gripped the stem of her wineglass. "Um, I guess."

"You don't know if your friends have kids?" he asked playfully, trying to ease this growing tension between them. "Or you don't have friends?"

Her eyelids lowered slightly, and her lips pursed together, as though she was about to deliver a scathing remark. Warmth flooded Marcus's bloodstream, and he wished he could take a picture of her in that exact second because she was absolutely gorgeous when she was in lecture mode.

"Of course I have friends." She didn't bother to hide the annoyance in her tone. But at least she was no longer trying to ignore him. "But the ones I spend the most time with don't usually bring their children with them to work."

"You mean your coworkers?" He wasn't sure if

he wanted to antagonize her or pity her right that second. "Don't you ever hang out with people outside the job?"

"I don't do much hanging out at all, Marcus. Or is this your way of asking me about my dating life?"

"Well, I wasn't asking about it specifically, but if you want to talk about it, we can." Although, he honestly didn't want to hear about any other guys who might be after her. He was sure there were plenty.

Before she could reply, though, his sons ran into the room with Aunt Freckles on their heels.

His aunt cupped her hand around her mouth and hollered, "Dinner's ready, gang!"

"Really, Freckles?" His mother chastised her former sister-in-law. "I've seen farmers call their pigs to the slop troughs with a more civilized tone."

"If you're more comfortable with me treating you like a pig, Sherilee, I'm happy to oblige." Freckles winked a bright blue eye-shadowed lid at Finn, who hooted with laughter at their mother's sputtering.

Finn and Freckles seemed to share the same desire to shock Sherilee King whenever the chance arose. And Marcus adored his aunt and his sister for it. Sure, he loved his mother, but the King matriarch needed to come off her high horse every now and then. As long as the two women didn't team up against him, he was fine.

"Now, now, ladies." Duke took their aunt's arm and twirled her toward the dining room, leaving Finn to walk with their frowning mother. "I've been waiting nearly five years for your famous chicken-fried steak, Freckles. I'm sure the only pig at the table will be me as I load up my plate."

Marcus's brother was the consummate peace-keeper of the family. He was the perfect son who could never fail at anything. Finn was always at-tempting to dethrone poor Duke from his good-natured pedestal with her smart-alecky comments and constant teasing, but he usually shrugged her off like a pesky fly.

"Hurry to your chair, before Dad gets there." Jack and Jordan each took one of Violet's hands in their own and tugged her toward the dining room. "He'll put all the mashed potatoes on his plate if you don't get some before him."

Violet threw a look over her shoulder at Marcus, a smirk tugging one corner of her lip upward. "Oh, he still does that?"

It wasn't until they were all seated at the table that he was able to defend himself. "What do you mean 'he still does that'?"

Instead of speaking directly to him, though, she told his sons, "One summer when we used to be in the Junior Diplomats Club, we were at a fancy state dinner for this group of foreign dignitaries and their children. The servers brought out our plates while I was still on the dance floor. When I got back to my seat, half of my potatoes au gratin were missing. Your dad denied it was him, but he still had cheese on his fork as he tried to quickly swallow down the evidence."

"What kind of junior diplomat steals food off someone else's plate at a state dinner?" Finn tsked, pretending to be scandalized.

"I was a sophomore in high school and going through a growth spurt. Besides, as I recall, Violet was so busy dancing with the French ambassador's son and swooning with the rest of the girls over his accent that I didn't think she'd notice."

Violet gasped. "You were jealous of Jean-Henri?"

At this point, everyone at the table was watching them, and Marcus hated being the center of attention. His incredulous sniff caused his chest to jut out in defiance. "No, I wasn't jealous of that guy. He might've had all the girls convinced he was a decent dancer, but he couldn't dribble a soccer ball to save his life. The European delegates lost the final match that year, and everyone probably forgot all about him after he flew back to Paris."

"You mean Jean-Henri Laurent?" Duke refilled Violet's wineglass. "He's a professional soccer player now. His team won the international finals last spring. So you must be the only one who forgot about him, big brother."

Violet laughed at that.

Dang. Now Marcus couldn't decide if she was more beautiful when she was angry or when she was laughing. Probably when she was angry because he could still remember her laughter when they were younger. But this level of heat was a new side to her he hadn't quite grown accustomed to.

Not that he was accustomed to seeing her at all lately. Luckily, he was able to sit across the table from her and silently study her as everyone else around them talked and argued and put on quite the display of squabbling and teasing.

He forgot how overwhelming his family could be to outsiders, although Violet wasn't technically an outsider. They'd spent many of their adolescent summers together, so she certainly had no trouble interjecting into the multiple conversations going on around the noisy table.

"So how long is everyone staying in town?" Violet asked.

"Well, I was hoping to return to my ship yesterday afternoon, but the former second lady over there—" Duke used his fork to gesture toward their mother at the head of the table "—made a call to one of her buddies at the Pentagon, and now my commanding officer insisted I take another week of leave."

Tessa, whose panic attack yesterday had resulted in quite a media scandal involving the handsome and heroic Special Agent Wyatt, buttered a freshly baked roll. "I was also supposed to be back in Washington today, but our strong-willed mother insisted that I stay on the ranch and keep a low profile. Hopefully, the press finds something new to interest them soon, and I can leave in a couple of days."

"I'm not going anywhere," Finn said around a

mouthful of fresh green beans. "I live on the Twin Kings, and I oversee the cattle operation. Which surprisingly lowers our mother's ability to control my life."

"How? I live on the ranch, too," Marcus pointed out. "Yet that doesn't stop Mom from her attempts to interfere in *my* job."

"I'm not interfering *or* controlling." His self-proclaimed vegan mother scraped her fork along her gravy-smeared plate with a bit too much force. "I'm simply orchestrating better options for my children."

"What about you, Aunt Freckles?" Violet smoothly shifted the subject before all the King siblings could voice their objections to their mother's careful re-phrasing of history. "I heard you have a successful restaurant in Sugar Falls now. When do you have to go back to Idaho?"

"Oh, I'm here for as long as my kiddos need me," Freckles explained as she passed a second gravy boat containing the untouched vegan version to Uncle Rider. He sniffed it then grimaced before passing it off to Sherilee.

Marcus's uncle twisted an end of his bushy gray mustache and winked at his estranged wife. "And here I thought you were staying because you couldn't get enough of me and my skills in the bed—"

"Whoa, you two!" Finn interrupted. "There are young children present."

Marcus tossed his white linen napkin onto his

plate in surrender. "That's probably my cue to get the boys home."

A defiant crease appeared between Jack's tired eyes. "But we want to hear more about the famous soccer player Violet got to dance with."

"He wasn't famous when Violet danced with him," Marcus said before realizing how petulant he sounded. "It was way back when we were still in high school."

"Did you and my dad go to school together?" Jordan asked Violet.

"No, I went to a boarding school near Washington, DC, and your dad went to Teton Ridge High."

"So then, how did you used to hang out all the time if you lived in different places?" Marcus could see the wheels spinning in Jordan's mind.

"We actually only saw each other once or twice a year at these boring events for children of politicians. Your dad and I were mostly pen pals."

"What's a pen pal?" Jack asked before using his sleeve to wipe the fruit punch off his upper lip.

"It's someone who lives far away, but you keep in touch by exchanging correspondence with them," Violet said, likely not realizing that she was speaking to a six-year-old with a limited vocabulary.

"What's *correspondence*?" Jack clearly wasn't letting up.

Jordan stage-whispered to his twin, "That means Dad slid into her DMs."

Several gasps came from the adults at the table

while Finn snorted rather loudly. MJ finally looked up from his phone with a huge grin across his face. Apparently, the boys' vocabulary wasn't as limited as it should be.

Marcus jerked his head sideways at his little brother. "I'm assuming you're the one who taught my impressionable children that expression?"

MJ's grin immediately turned into a snarl. "So now you're blaming me for that, too?"

Violet sat up straighter, as though she was going to defend her client from Marcus's latest allegations. But before she could launch her opening defense, Finn made a chopping motion with her palm, like a referee trying to break up a fight.

"It was me, Marcus," Finn said with an unapologetic grin. "The boys overheard me and Freckles talking about… Well, suffice it to say that we didn't know they were listening."

"What's a dang *DM*?" Uncle Rider asked, causing another snort from Finn.

"It means *direct message*, you old coot." Freckles rolled her eyes. "When you're interested in talking to someone on social media, but you don't want everyone seeing what you write, you slide into that person's direct messages. That way you can have a private conversation."

"Well, nobody better be sliding into *your* DMs," Rider told Freckles, not picking up on the fact that the twins still only understood the literal definition instead of the more commonly known flirtatious implication. "You're still a married woman. Technically."

"Are *you* married, Violet?" Jordan asked.

She took a rather long gulp of her wine, and Marcus realized he was holding his own breath waiting for her to answer. Finally, she shook her head. "No, I'm not married."

"Do you have kids?" Jack asked next and Marcus's heart twisted.

"Boys, it's not polite to ask so many personal questions," he quietly cautioned his sons. Especially when Marcus already knew the painful answer.

"It's okay." Violet's half-hearted smile didn't quite reach her sad eyes. "I appreciate their curiosity. No, I do not currently have any children."

They still hadn't really talked about the babies they'd lost, and Marcus swallowed the guilt rising in his throat.

"Do you ever slide into anyone's DMs?" Jordan asked, causing Marcus to nearly choke.

"I go out on dates occasionally. But I'm usually too busy with work and don't have much time for social media."

Ah ha! It only took forty-five minutes of uncomfortable family bantering and an inquisition by a couple of six-year-olds to get the answer she'd dodged earlier.

"Dad says he's too busy to go out on dates, too," Jack replied. "He used to be married to our mom, but now he's called a widow. Like the black poisonous spider."

"Widower," Jordan corrected.

"Yeah," Jack nodded. "He's like a black widower, but not poisonous. So that means that you can slide into his DMs again if you wanted to."

This time, Finn wasn't the only one at the table who snorted. Even diplomatic Duke didn't bother to hide his laughter. Marcus thought he was immune to being embarrassed by his family, but a flame of heat seared the skin of his neck and shot to his face.

Violet toyed with her macaroni necklace, causing the paint to smear on her fingers and her white blouse. She didn't seem to notice, though, because her eyes were too busy darting from the faces of his eager sons back to his.

Great. She was probably thinking this was some sort of setup. That he was a lonely, single father using his kids to pick up women because he couldn't get a date on his own. In fact, he'd had plenty of offers from plenty of women, but with two young sons at home, the timing just never felt right. He wanted to set the record straight; however, it had been a long day, and he was on the verge of saying something that Violet could later hold against him.

"Okay, nobody is sliding into anyone's DMs. Boys, thank your aunt Freckles for a lovely dinner. You have school tomorrow, and we still have to go over your math worksheet before bedtime."

Or before his family came up with more random

comments that would make Marcus seem additionally ridiculous and pathetic. Violet already thought badly enough of him as it was.

Unfortunately, he couldn't quite subdue that unexplainable need to prove himself to her. As his sons were making their way around the table distracting his family with goodbye hugs, Marcus stopped behind Violet's chair on the way out and lowered his head until his mouth was level with her ear.

He heard her sharp intake of breath, then whispered, "Just so you know, I'm not some sorry sack who can't get a date. I'm just careful with who I bring home to meet my over-the-top family."

Her head tilted slightly, but she didn't turn to look at him. Probably a good call considering her lips weren't all that far from his as she replied somewhat breathlessly, "It's none of my business, either way."

"Well, I'm making it your business. You said you like to have all the facts, and those are the facts." He couldn't stop the suggestive tone creeping into his voice as he added a parting shot. "Use that information however you see fit, counselor."

Chapter Five

"There's just not a lot of room at Gan Gan's house right now," Marcus told his sons Tuesday morning when they asked why they had to remain with him at the cabin for the whole week. In reality, even with Tessa and Aunt Freckles temporarily staying there, there was plenty of room. The truth was Marcus didn't want to keep running into Violet.

Besides, the cabin wasn't really a cabin at all. It was a house of nearly three thousand square feet in a secluded area less than a mile from the main driveway on the Twin Kings Ranch. And technically, it was their home. Marcus and Brie had built it right before their wedding, and everything inside—from the custom-designed drawer pulls on the kitchen cabinets to the floral upholstered rocker in the den—had been picked out by his wife.

Twice now, he'd been embarking on what he'd thought was a new journey with a woman he loved, eager to share his life with someone. And twice those relationships had ended in disaster. Different journeys and different disasters, obviously. Yet both times he'd had to move forward on his own, which was always easier if he didn't look back at what he'd lost.

He'd thought about redecorating a few times, to make it seem like less of a shrine to his late wife; however, he'd never gotten around to making any changes. Partly because Marcus had needed so much help with the pair of toddlers—and managing his grief—after Brie had passed away.

As a single dad, he'd become increasingly dependent on his family for backup. His sister Dahlia, who lived in town and had a five-year-old daughter, usually picked up the twins after school and brought them to his office. Uncle Rider loved entertaining the boys with riding lessons and old rodeo stories, and Finn was always happy to keep an eye on her nephews whenever Marcus had to work late.

Although, his youngest sister's inappropriate sense of humor was proving to be more of a bad influence now that the kids were repeating the outlandish things she said. And then there was Marcus's mother, who was a little *too* supportive when she was in town for occasional visits. Now that his father was gone, it was time to accept the fact that Sherilee King had returned to Wyoming full-time. She doted on her grandkids even as she drove her own children crazy with her unsolicited opinions and high-handed interference in every aspect of their lives.

"But everyone at Gan Gan's will miss us," Jack pointed out.

"I'm sure they'll get used to it." Marcus looked at the twins' pouting faces in his rearview mirror. "We have a perfectly good house that nobody is using, and you guys are getting old enough to ride your bicycles to the main house to visit whenever you feel like it."

"I don't like my plain ol' bike anymore." Jack crossed his arms under the shoulder strap of his seat belt. "It doesn't go as fast as a 50cc-engine motocross dirt bike would."

"Motorcycles are dangerous," Jordan reminded his brother for the hundredth time.

"Only if you crash them."

"Jack, you crash everything." His twin wasn't wrong. Jack was not only impulsive, he was also the most accident-prone child in the history of Teton Ridge Elementary School. And he was still in the first grade. The school nurse had Marcus on speed dial. They'd taken so many trips to the nearby hospital for sprains, stitches and casts, the staff informally referred to the pediatric exam room as the Jack King Suite.

Sure, Jordan first took an interest in medical conditions after learning about the cause of his mother's untimely death. But then Jack's frequent visits to urgent-care offices and emergency rooms really took that fascination to a whole new level.

"Aunt Finn said she'd teach us how to drive a Polaris," Jack said, referring to the smaller all-terrain vehicles the ranch hands sometimes used for hauling supplies. "Could we get one for me and Jordan to drive to the main house? I'll wear a helmet."

"I'm not riding with you on an ATV." Jordan shook his head. "Even if Dad says yes, I won't go. Not even with a helmet."

"Fine, then." Jack stuck out his tongue at his brother before plopping his elbow on his windowsill, stubbornly cupping his chin in his hand. "I'll just take my slow, boring bike to the main house to see Violet then."

"Why do you want to visit Violet so badly?" Marcus asked as he pulled his SUV into the drop-off line at the elementary school.

"Because she doesn't ever get to be around kids," Jack said, as though that explained everything.

Marcus reached for the stainless-steel travel mug in his center cupholder. He was going to need a lot more coffee this morning to decipher the logic of an almost-seven-year-old. "So you think you two are doing her a favor by rewarding her with your presence?"

"Gan Gan says we're a delight," Jordan replied, not picking up on the sarcasm. "And Aunt Freckles says being around us keeps her on her toes. Don't you think Violet wants to be on her toes?"

Suddenly, Marcus flashed back to a memory of the summer before his senior year in high school. He and Violet and two thousand other so-called junior global ambassadors had been invited to attend the International Summit at Sea. The event sounded prestigious but really was just a bunch of teenagers attending lectures and seminars all day on a cruise ship anchored in international waters with no cellphone service. He and Violet had been so bored with the evening's organized activities that they'd snuck off in search of an adventure and stumbled upon the ship's beauty salon, which had been closed since there weren't any paying customers on that particular trip. There'd been a bet—for the life of him, he couldn't remember what it was—and he'd lost and had had to paint Violet's toenails for her.

Social Scene Red.

That had been the color she'd selected from the wall of nail polishes. Unfortunately, the end result looked more like Crime Scene Red after he'd made a sloppy mess with his too-big fingers and the way-too-tiny brush. But Violet had only laughed and proudly worn her flip-flops the rest of the weekend, showing off those smudged red toenails like they were works of art.

Now, all these years later, it finally occurred to Marcus that Violet hadn't been proud of his paint job. She'd been proud of winning whatever bet they'd had. Had she always been this competitive and he'd never noticed it? He was still wracking his brain for the terms of that wager when a horn blasted behind them.

All the cars in front of him had pulled forward, and the crossing guard was waving for him to follow along. Most of the time he parked and walked the boys to their classroom. But yesterday, Jordan had commented on how all the big kids got dropped off at the curb. Now Jack was begging for a motorcycle, of all things. What would they ask for tomorrow? Probably a six pack of beer. Or, in Jordan's case, a 401(k) plan.

Why did it feel like his babies were in such a hurry to grow up? And why did the realization suddenly make him feel so lonely?

Sighing, Marcus put the SUV in Park and turned to give them each an awkward half hug through the narrow opening separating the front seat from the back seat. "Good luck on your spelling tests. And eat the celery sticks I packed in your lunch."

"Did you put peanut butter and raisins on them like Aunt Freckles does?" Jack, the picky eater, asked. Thankfully, they weren't trying to grow up too fast.

"Yes," Marcus said, trying not to think of how old the raisins he'd found in the cabin's cupboard were. He really needed to go to the market instead of picking up last-minute supplies from the pantry in the main house like he'd done last night. "Don't forget. Aunt Dahlia is picking you guys up again today."

He gave the boys a final wave before driving to the county building that housed both the courthouse and the annexed sheriff's station. Deputy Broman had just returned from his overnight patrol shift, still sporting the black eye from MJ's attempts to resist arrest. The man was also still carrying a decade-old grudge from the safety academy when Marcus had beat him out as the top-scoring recruit, earning the Chief's Commendation Award at their graduation. Things hadn't improved in their professional relationship when Marcus had later won the election for county sheriff in a landslide and become Broman's boss.

Despite his deputy's attitude toward Marcus, though, the man was a dedicated cop and followed procedure by the book. He also knew how to write an ironclad arrest report that Violet, or any other attorney, would be hard-pressed to dispute in the courtroom.

"Morning, Broman," Marcus said as he used his electronic key card to open the secured back door only accessible to employees. "Uneventful shift, I hope?"

"As much as can be expected. It'll be nice when all those media vans camped outside the Twin Kings get whatever story they came for and leave." Broman had been complaining about the influx of news reporters snooping around town since before the funeral. Each time he commented on it, Marcus heard the underlying implication that it was somehow the King family's fault that the department's limited staff and even more limited budget had to be stretched thin to cover the additional patrol duties. Luckily, most of the local shops and restaurants appreciated the extra business, though. "Oh, and we got a noise complaint about Jay Grover again. Apparently he fired his fourth divorce attorney and went on another Taylor Swift binge. The neighbors are getting pretty tired of him getting drunk and blasting bad breakup songs at three in the morning. He was already passed out by the time I got there, and his Bluetooth speaker battery had died, so I left it for you guys on the day shift to handle."

"Okay. I have a few calls to make this morning, and then I'll drive over to Grover's house and have another chat with him. Speaking of lawyers, though, MJ's defense attorney is meeting the prosecutor here this afternoon to look at the body-cam footage from the night of his arrest. Can you make sure the toxicology reports are printed out before you leave?"

"No problem." Broman shifted his gear bag higher onto his shoulder as he passed through the door and inside the building. "Hey, is it true that your baby brother's lawyer is also your ex-girlfriend?"

Marcus clenched the door handle tighter before forcing his fingers to relax. It was bad enough that his law-enforcement duties were suddenly completely at odds with his brotherly duties, and that no matter what he did in this situation, someone would be pissed at him. Yet now he had the unfortunate bonus of dealing with Violet, on top of an already-precarious balancing act. All he could manage was a tense nod of acknowledgment before he retreated to his office.

The bulk of Marcus's morning was spent dealing with a sullen and hungover Jay Grover; pulling over the mayor's wife to give her another ticket for blowing through the new stop sign at Frontier Drive and Stampede Boulevard; responding to a call at Burnworth's Bakery where Mrs. Crenshaw was refusing to leave until Mr. Burnworth, the notoriously temperamental baker, honored an expired coupon for 50 percent off a blueberry muffin; and explaining to Mr. Watterson at the Weathered W Ranch that his overweight pygmy goat (and not a rogue gang—as he had called them—of vegan teenagers) was responsible for tearing up his vegetable garden.

At one o'clock, Marcus grabbed a chicken sandwich to go at Biscuit Betty's, then buried himself in his office to finish reviewing operation reports from the prior weekend. Next, he went through his employees' time sheets and approved the overtime pay for the extra shifts they'd had to pull for all the Secret Service task-force meetings and security briefings related to the funeral. Due to Tessa's little media scandal with Agent Wyatt and all the lingering news agencies sticking around, his deputies had earned some hefty overtime checks this week.

By the time Rod D'Agostino, the front-desk volunteer, announced Violet's arrival, Marcus was already regretting his decision to hold this particular meeting at the station.

"The DA called to say he can't make it, but that other attorney is here." Rod had been a homicide detective in Chicago before retiring and moving to Teton Ridge with his wife, who wanted to get away from the big city. Unfortunately, the small-town life didn't hold much interest for an old-school cop like Rod, and Mrs. D'Agostino was so sick of listening to true-crime podcasts at home, she'd begged Marcus to let her husband volunteer at the station a few days a week.

"The junior cadets from the high-school program are holding their monthly training in the community room," Rod reminded him. "Do you want me to put her in the interrogation room? I can come in there with you as your backup in case she gets a little slippery with all that fancy lawyer talk."

"It's called the interview room," he corrected Rod, who was clearly missing his days as a detective on the police force. "And since we aren't charging her with any crimes, it's probably safe enough for me to meet with her in my office."

"Suit yourself." Rod shrugged. "I'll be out here listening to the feds on the encrypted scanner if you need me."

As he straightened his desk, Marcus made a mental note to call the Secret Agent in charge at the ranch and advise him that Rod had figured out how to hack their frequency.

When Violet walked in, Marcus almost dropped the stack of time sheets he'd just signed. Someone must have sent her some clothes, because the outfit she had on definitely wasn't from Sherilee King's closet.

The silky-smooth fabric of the black pants hugged every curve, from the low-riding waistband all the way down to the cropped ankle length, showing off spiky five-inch heels. The matching jacket was fitted and hinted at being professional if it wasn't for the daring V-neck of the blouse under the four buttons holding the outer garment closed.

Technically, one might be able to call the articles of clothing a business suit. But the way Violet wore it gave Marcus very unbusinesslike thoughts.

"What's wrong?" Violet immediately asked. "Your nostrils are all round and huffy, like you can't get enough air."

Marcus sniffed and shook his head. "Uh, nothing. I was just thinking that your outfit doesn't look like anything I've seen in a courtroom. At least not here in Ridgecrest County."

"Considering the fact that our judge was wearing sneakers and basketball pants under his robe at the last hearing, I'll consider myself overdressed. Besides, only one box of my clothes arrived and the dressiest material in Finn's closet is flannel. I had to borrow this shirt from your aunt Freckles."

That certainly explained the plunging V-neck. Marcus shook his head to clear it.

Violet placed her briefcase on the floor and gestured to the chair across from his desk, reminding him of his manners.

He extended his hand. "Sorry. Please have a seat."

She sat down and crossed her legs, drawing his attention to the high heels that would become highly impractical as soon as the next snow fell. Her shoes made him think of her toes, which made him think of what nail-polish color she had on underneath, and before he could stop himself he blurted out, "What was the bet that I lost?"

She lifted both eyebrows. "You're going to have to narrow that down for me. You used to lose bets to me all the time."

He frowned. "First of all, that's highly unlikely, since I rarely take bets that I might lose. Second, I'm talking about the one at that Summit at Sea cruise. Right before our senior year in high school. Remember that empty beauty salon?"

Violet's cheeks turned an adorable shade of pink, and she quickly busied herself with searching for something in her briefcase. "Are we here to talk about some old bet or about your brother's case?"

"Well, we *were* going to talk about the case. But now that it's obvious you're trying to avoid the subject, I would much rather discuss that bet."

"Fine." She finally dragged her eyes to his. "We'd snuck off from that global pyramid team-building

workshop, and you were making fun of me for bringing my Shirley Temple with me."

"That's right! They closed all the bars on the ship
and were only serving preapproved mocktails. I remember my roommate was the Secretary of State's
son. He smuggled a bottle of tequila in his suitcase
and was charging kids to spike their drinks. So did
I dare you to chug it or something?"

"No. You bet me that I couldn't tie a knot into the
stem of a cherry. With my tongue."

Now he felt the heat rise to his own cheeks. And
other parts of his body, as well. He remembered her
skillful mouth and her agile tongue oh so well, and
his body was responding as if he was eighteen all
over again.

As if to drive him further to distraction, she
opened her soft lips ever so slightly and let out a
breathy sigh. Her next words snapped him right back
to the present, though.

"So am I here to talk about a past bet you lost to
me, or am I here to talk about a *current* case your
absent prosecutor is going to lose to me?"

Violet would've had to be blind not to see how
uncomfortable Marcus was as he shifted his weight
in his office chair. His eyes kept dropping to her
mouth, and despite their growing animosity toward
each other, the attraction was clearly still there. Her
stomach did a little dance at the realization that she
was having such a physical effect on the man who

had let it be known to everyone at the ranch that he didn't enjoy having Violet in town.

The only time she ever used her looks or her femininity to gain the upper hand—either in her personal life or in her career, which took up most of her personal life—was when she wanted to lure some good ol' boy attorney into underestimating her. Then she could strike when they weren't paying attention and win an argument or even an entire case.

It was tempting to use the same strategy against Marcus because all his focus seemed to be on the personal history between them. He might want to secure the upper hand in some sort of imagined verbal battle between them, but that desire was distracting him from the only issue that mattered.

MJ.

She cleared her throat. "So I hear you have a body-cam video of my client that the prosecutor is planning to introduce as evidence."

"Yes." Marcus straightened his already-straight shoulders. "Along with witness testimony."

"Who is the witness?"

He rubbed the back of his neck before admitting, "Kendra Broman."

Violet frowned. "The daughter of the deputy who made the arrest?"

"She's also MJ's girlfriend."

"So you're admitting she has divided loyalties. Why would she be willing to testify against her boyfriend?"

"She's not testifying *against* him," Marcus tried to reason. "She's only testifying to what she saw."

"Was Kendra drinking that night?" Violet asked rhetorically. She knew the answer because MJ had admitted as much to her.

Marcus straightened some already-neat papers on his desk. "I believe the arrest report implies that she was."

"Right. The arrest report that her father wrote. Interesting that there was no Breathalyzer done on her, yet there was one done on my client. So how much did Kendra drink that night? How often does she normally drink? And with whom? Has her dad ever caught her drinking before? How does her dad feel about her dating MJ? Has she ever heard her father talking about his distaste for my client or for my client's family?" Violet paused only long enough to let her rapid-fire questions sink in. "Do you see where I'm going with this, Marcus? If the prosecution puts Kendra on the witness stand, I'm going to have to ask her these questions. In public and under oath. She's barely eighteen and in love with a boy her father disapproves of. We both remember how that feels. Don't make me put Kendra through a cross-examination when the body camera can deliver the exact same evidence."

Marcus studied her, the deepened crease above his nose highlighting his serious blue eyes. "Your father disapproved of me?"

Of course that was the part of her speech he focused on. Violet rolled her eyes. "No, my dad adored you. It was my mom who had an issue with our relationship. Although, to be honest, she would've disapproved of me having *any* boyfriend that distracted me from my future prospects. She still does."

"Well, she got what she wanted in the end, didn't she?"

Violet swallowed down the sting. "You mean when I miscarried her grandchildren? Or when she had to take an emergency absence from the Senate to take care of me when I was on bed rest for two weeks afterward? She never left my side, crying whenever she thought I was asleep. I know what she said to your dad that day was unconscionable, but she was also the person who told me not to be disappointed with you, Marcus. She reminded me that you were going through a lot of stress with boot camp, dealing with the added worry that you were risking your life joining the military. I know you don't like my mother, Marcus, but even she's not that much of a monster."

He shoved a hand through his short hair. "No. God, no. I just meant that her plan for you and your life wasn't derailed too much by our relationship after all."

"Derailed?" The stinging sensation didn't go away. "That's how you want to describe what happened? I was in the hospital for three days, and the father of my children never so much as called." She held up a hand when he opened his mouth. "Yeah, I know you didn't get my letter. But learning that now doesn't lessen the pain I felt back then."

"I felt plenty of pain back then, too, Violet."

She sucked in a deep breath, but the air between them was so thick with tension, it didn't bring her any clarity. "Listen, we can't keep bringing up our past every time we see each other. We're both here to do a job. Even if we can't agree on how the other should do *their* job, we should at least agree to put on our professional pants and try to act civil. For MJ's sake."

His eyes dropped to her hips, then traveled slowly down her legs. "You call those your professional pants?"

A jolt of electricity shot through her limbs, and she immediately stood up as though she could shake away the feeling.

"What's wrong with these pants?" Following his gaze, she ran her hands along her hips to check for rips or stains. His soft groan was barely audible, making her suddenly realize his issue. "Wait. You haven't suddenly become ultramodest in your old age?"

"No. Of course not. I just meant that it was easier to think of you a certain way when you were wearing my mother's clothes."

"What a woman wears shouldn't affect how you think of her."

"I know that. And if you were any other woman, keeping my thoughts under control wouldn't be an issue. Unfortunately, I have the privilege of already knowing exactly what is under those pants. So it's a lot more difficult setting those kinds of thoughts aside when my brain and that tight fabric is so intent on reminding me."

A shiver raced through Violet at his admission, and instead of retreating and putting some distance between them, she took a step forward and placed her hands on his desk. "You think you're the only one who has to deal with thinking about what someone looks like under their clothes?"

That didn't exactly come out the way she'd intended, which made her all the more defensive.

He stood and adjusted his black leather duty belt. "You mean my county-issued uniform I'm required to wear for my job?"

"Uniforms are supposed to fit…well…uniformly. But your biceps look like they're going to bust through the sleeves at the slightest flex. And unlike you, I don't have the luxury of already knowing what's under that polyester-blend fabric because you clearly weren't bench-pressing as much back when we were eighteen."

This time, his groan was louder when he stepped around his desk. Violet's brain was shooting up all the red flags it could muster, but her legs were acting of their own accord. Before she knew it, she'd met him halfway and was in his arms, her lips pressed to his.

Oh, hell. She was kissing Marcus King.

Again.

It felt so familiar and yet so new and thrilling all at the same time. They had been each other's first so many years ago, learning how to kiss with just the right amount of pressure and curiosity. Clearly, their mouths hadn't forgotten all those stolen minutes of practice and eagerly molded together as their tongues made up for lost time.

His hands spanned around her waist, and her fingers dug into his shoulders as the rest of her body melted against his. She sighed as he angled his head and deepened the kiss. He tasted like coffee and misspent youth, and she was at risk of drowning in that familiar passion all over again.

She pulled away only slightly, needing to give herself a second to think about what had just happened. Her heartbeat pounded in her ears as his warm breath fanned her forehead.

"God, was it always this good between us?" he asked, resting his lips against her temple.

"I think so." She shuddered, letting her palms slide down to his defined pectoral muscles. "But we were both so young back then and didn't know anything else. I remember being able to feel your heart beating in double-time against my skin, just like it is now. Except we were usually wearing a lot less clothing. And there wasn't usually this coming between us."

Tucking his chin, Marcus watched as Violet's finger traced along one of the points of the star-shaped badge on his chest. She lifted her face to his and was about to pick up where they'd left off when an announcement blared over the intercom.

"We gotta Code Twin heading your way, Sheriff."

Chapter Six

Marcus had only seconds to jump away from Violet before his office door busted open and Jack spilled the contents of his rocket-ship backpack all over the floor. Jordan was right behind with their aunt Dahlia and little Amelia bringing up the rear.

"Oh, hi, Violet." Jack smiled before dropping to the floor to collect his scattered belongings. "I didn't know you would be here."

Violet smoothed her slightly tousled hair and blinked several times. "I, uh, didn't know I'd be staying this long."

"Why're your lips all red, Dad?" Jordan asked as his brother shoved a handful of crumpled-up papers and a half-eaten banana back into his backpack. "Do you have a fever?"

"Or did you get a frozen slushy at the Mighty Mart?" Jack, whose brain went to sugar before medical conditions, was now intently staring at him, as well. "I thought Mrs. Contreras said they were out of the cherry flavor."

"Uh, no," Marcus said before dragging the back of his hand across the lower half of his face. Judging by the absence of any lipstick left on Violet's full lips, he knew exactly why his mouth was so red. And so did his sister.

Dahlia gave a little snort before depositing a lunch box in the shape of a T. rex on the chair. "Sorry to interrupt what must be an important and, by the looks of it, very *professional* meeting. But Amelia has her ballet lesson in about five minutes, and she refuses to do her pirouettes when her cousins are there to distract her."

"I don't blame her." Marcus winked at his niece, then shot his sister a warning look. "Obnoxious family members getting all up in your business are the worst."

Steering her daughter toward the door, Dahlia paused and looked back over her shoulder. "Hey, Violet. Tessa and Finn are coming by Big Millie's for happy hour this evening if you need a girls' night out."

"Can we come?" Jordan asked his aunt.

"Then it wouldn't be a girls' night out." Dahlia

wiggled her eyebrows. "Maybe your dad could take you guys to get a slushy at the Mighty Mart, instead. He looks like he could use a bit of cooling down."

When their aunt had left the office, Jack turned to Marcus. "But I wanna go with Violet to happy hour."

"Oh, I don't know if I'm going yet," Violet replied before Marcus could. "I have a lot of work to do."

"To keep Uncle MJ out of Daddy's jail?" Jordan asked.

"That's right," Violet nodded.

The back of Marcus's throat vibrated as he swallowed down a frustrated groan. "For the record, I'm trying to keep Uncle MJ out of my jail, too. And any future jails. By teaching him a lesson."

"You mean like when Coach makes us run extra laps when we mess up at soccer practice?" Jordan asked.

"Yeah, kind of like that."

"How does that teach you not to mess up?" Violet's smooth forehead, the one he'd just pressed his own against, creased with confusion. "It seems like it would only make you tired and prone to make more mistakes."

Marcus shook his head. "But if there aren't consequences for your actions, what's to stop you from making the same mistakes over and over again?"

"How about having a patient coach or mentor or maybe even…oh, I don't know—" Violet dramatically shrugged her shoulders "—say, a big brother who *guides* you and steers you in the right direction?"

"So this is my fault?" Marcus crossed his arms across his chest and tried to ignore the way her eyes widened at his biceps. Remembering her earlier admission, he flexed his muscles slightly. "I'm supposed to be *babysitting* MJ, in addition to dealing with the rest of my family's antics? All while working sixty-plus hours a week at my job and raising my kids on my own?"

Violet's gaze snapped back to his face. Possibly at the reminder that he was a single dad. "Nobody said *babysitting*."

"Keegan's mom did," Jordan announced out of the blue. "At the bake sale, I heard her tell the other parents that you needed to hire a real babysitter so you could go out with a real woman like her."

Violet arched a brow at Marcus, and he resisted the urge to tug at his collar as he explained, "Their friend Keegan's mom has been very determined lately to get me to join this little group she formed called Single Socials. It's not really my scene, though. Just in case you thought it was."

"From what MJ tells me, you don't have much of a social scene at all." Violet smirked, and Marcus silently cursed his baby brother for opening his big mouth.

"I told Ms. Parker we didn't need a babysitter because we weren't babies," Jack said, while balancing on his knees in his father's office chair and spinning fast in circles. "But then she said that all grown-ups need to spend alone time with other grown-ups."

"You're a grown-up and a real woman," Jordan told Violet. "Maybe you should spend alone time with my dad."

After the DM-sliding conversation the other night, Marcus should've been immune to his sons' embarrassing announcements. He wasn't. And neither, apparently, was Violet. Her eyes went wide, and her mouth opened and closed several times as her face went nearly crimson. Ha. That's what she got for implying that he needed to socialize more.

"Actually, uh, your father and I, uh, have already spent plenty of alone time together for the day," she finally managed.

Marcus's mind immediately skipped back to the kiss that had been interrupted when the boys had arrived. He cleared his throat and added, "In fact, it'd probably be better if we didn't spend any alone time together at all."

Her head gave the slightest twitch, as though his words had stunned her. Hell, he'd stunned himself with the harshness of his statement. But the truth was that he couldn't trust himself around her. And if he wanted to keep her at a distance, then it was better that he maintain some sort of battle line between them.

"You're probably right." Violet's smile was polite, but her eyes held a note of calculation. "After all, I already accomplished what I came here to do."

She said goodbye to the twins and was gone for a full five minutes before Marcus realized he'd might've just been played. It was two hours later when he confirmed it.

Marcus had been so distracted by Violet's visit to his office, he'd driven the boys home without remembering to stop at the grocery store. He was standing in front of the still-empty fridge contemplating going to the bunkhouse for dinner when his cell phone rang.

"So I just had an interesting chat with defense counsel in your brother's case." Reed Nakamoto, the prosecutor who hadn't shown for the meeting earlier today, jumped right into it. "I thought you said she was your *ex*-girlfriend."

"I don't think I said either way." At least not to Reed or to anyone else. But small-town news traveled fast. "Why? What's up?"

"Well, Miss Cortez-Hill seems to think that you and she have some kind of understanding. That you're on the same page and don't want me calling Kendra Broman as a witness."

"I don't know if I'd call it the same page." Marcus swung the fridge door closed, annoyed that he didn't even have so much as an expired bottle of beer in there. "Violet made some good points about the damaging effects it could have on Kendra if she has to suffer an embarrassing cross-examination."

Reed tsked. "I told you from the get-go that there was a lot of potential for conflicts of interest in this case, Marcus. You insisted we treat your brother the same way we would treat any other defendant and not give him any special favors. So I'm going to insist that you don't do any more favors for your pretty little girlfriend without running them by me first."

"I didn't do anyone a favor, and I didn't agree to anything. She came to see the body-cam footage, a meeting that you were supposed to attend, by the way." If Reed had been there, there definitely wouldn't have been any heated looks or make-out sessions.

"Yeah, sorry about that. I ran into Judge Calhoun at Biscuit Betty's, and a group of us headed over to the rec center for a game of three on three."

So the DA shooting hoops with the judge in the case wasn't considered a conflict of interest, but the sheriff meeting with the defense attorney in a county office was? Small-town boundaries were more of a suggestion than a written rule, but the man was right. Marcus had always done things by the book, and he didn't appreciate anyone suggesting the hint of impropriety. Even if the one doing the suggesting was doing the same thing or worse.

Marcus pinched the bridge of his nose. "Anyway, Miss Cortez-Hill brought up not needing Kendra's witness testimony, and I didn't agree or disagree. That was the gist of our meeting."

Well, that wasn't exactly it. Other things had happened in that office, as well, but Reed didn't need to know all of that.

"Okay, good. Just between you and me, the defense counsel is probably right. In this instance. But we need to be careful with these big-city attorneys coming into town and sweet-talking us into deals."

"Nobody's sweet-talking me, Reed."

Marcus's fingers were gripping the cell phone so hard, it was a wonder the thing hadn't snapped in half before he could disconnect the call. Normally, he was proud of his department's three-year record for not having any complaints or lawsuits filed against them due to deputy misconduct. He wasn't about to have his ethical standards called into question because his ex-girlfriend had distracted him before going over his head to get what she wanted.

Right now, he needed a burger, he needed a beer and he needed to have a few words with Violet Cortez-Hill, Esquire.

"Come on, boys," Marcus called down the hallway, grabbing his coat. He might have to forego the beer since he didn't want to waste time changing out of his uniform. "We're gonna go to Aunt Dahlia's and crash the girls' night out party."

After leaving Marcus's office, Violet had gone straight to the tiny one-room law library in the basement of the courthouse building. The phone reception down there must've been terrible because her phone pinged to life with notifications as soon as the elevator doors opened onto the lobby floor two hours later.

The first voice mail was from her mom. She could listen to that later. She tapped on the screen to hear the second message, which had just come in fifteen minutes ago. "Hi there, Miss Cortez-Hill. It's Reed Nakamoto calling you back again. Listen, I just got off the phone with Sheriff King and, as much as I'm willing to cut young MJ a deal and avoid a trial, I just don't think I'm gonna be able to get the sheriff on board. Let's talk more tomorrow and see if we can find some common ground."

It could be that Reed was just that bad at plea deals, trying to play the good cop to Marcus's bad cop. Or it could be that Marcus was seriously being this stubborn. Probably it was a little bit of both. Either way, she wasn't in favor of any deals that didn't include the dismissal of all charges. And if she could ever get Marcus and the district attorney in the same room together, she'd tell them both exactly that.

Clenching her jaw in frustration, Violet was really in no mood to deal with her mom's message at the moment. Yet as she shoved open the heavy door leading outside to the courthouse steps, she couldn't stop the uneasy feeling that something was wrong. That there might be some sort of accident or emergency, since her mother usually only texted between their weekly calls. Sighing, she put the phone back to her ear.

"Hey, angel. It's Mom. I was just thinking that once my campaign kicks off in a couple of weeks, I'm not going to have much time off. What do you think of a girls' trip? Remember that time we took off and went to Punta Cana? Just the two of us? That was fun." It was also the first June after the miscarriage, and her mom had known that it would be a difficult time for her daughter since summers had always been a big deal for Violet and Marcus. "Anyway, look at your schedule and get back to my aide, Yvonne, with your availability. Oh, and maybe we should bring Senator Valdivia with us. She has a daughter your age and, coincidentally, has just been appointed chair of the senate judiciary committee. I told her you might be interested…"

Violet groaned, cutting off the message before the end. Her relationship with her mom was complicated, with equal parts of love and frustration. When Eva Cortez-Hill was being just a "normal mom," things were great. They could do regular mother-and-daughter things together—shopping, spa days, vacations—and they got along fine. But when her mom was being "the senator," she was nearly insufferable. The tricky part was knowing when one role was about to switch to the other so Violet could get out in time to save herself.

The old-fashioned streetlamps had just come on, and looking down Stampede Boulevard, Violet saw the vintage sign for Big Millie's Saloon in the distance. Yep, she definitely needed a cocktail after today's events. She also needed to vent to any King whose first name wasn't Marcus.

"Hi, Vi." Dahlia extended arms in welcome from behind the hundred-year-old refinished walnut bar she now owned and ran. "Let me get you a drink as a thanks for helping my baby brother out of his latest scrape with the law."

"Much to the annoyance of your *big* brother," Violet responded. "He isn't here, is he?"

"Not yet." Tessa smiled and patted the empty seat beside her.

Violet let out a deep breath as she plopped herself onto a gold leather–covered bar stool. She'd heard that the Wild West–era saloon and former brothel had been fully refurbished, but she was impressed with how Dahlia had managed to make the place seem trendy while keeping the decor true to its historic roots. "In that case, I'll take a glass of any wine you already have open."

Dahlia drew a bottle from under the bar, and Freckles breezed out of the kitchen carrying two double burgers loaded with every possible topping listed on the limited bar menu.

"Hey, Aunt Freckles," Violet said, immediately feeling more relaxed at the sight of the older woman's friendly face. "If I'd known you were here cooking, I would've left the courthouse earlier. Did Mrs. King kick you out of her kitchen?"

"No, darlin'." Freckles wore a crisp white apron over her tight zebra-print blouse and even tighter jeans. "I needed a break from Rider. That old coot has been getting a bit frisky lately. Trying to prove there's still a little gas left in his tank, if you know what I mean."

Marcus's three sisters covered their ears, despite the fact that they should've been well-accustomed to the older woman's candid comments.

"Aunt Freckles," Dahlia scolded as she lowered her cupped palms, "we can't unhear those sorts of things."

Violet hid her smile behind a large sip of wine while the King women continued to banter. Someone asked where Duke had gone, and she didn't have the heart to rat their brother out and admit that she'd seen him on her way into the building. He'd been standing outside the heavy oak front door, huddled under his puffy down jacket and quietly arguing with someone on his cell phone.

Violet's guest room at the ranch was next to Duke's, and two nights ago, she'd accidentally overheard him pleading with someone on a video call to let him be the one to tell Tom what had happened. Her interest had obviously been piqued, but then her own phone had rung with an incoming video call from her mom, and she'd spent the next ten minutes strategically holding the camera lens at an angle that wouldn't give away her location.

Not that she was keeping her presence on the Twin Kings a secret from her mother. In fact, it could be that her mom already knew something was up and that's why she'd called again today with the idea for a mother-daughter vacation. Guilt. She was still processing Marcus's claim about the senator leading him to believe Violet had had an abortion all those years ago, and she wasn't yet sure how she wanted to confront her mom. Until then, Violet wasn't going to mention the name Marcus to either of her parents.

As if her thoughts had summoned the man, Marcus's twin boys tore through the entrance of Big Millie's.

"We're here for girls' night," Jordan said by way of greeting.

"Will you watch our jackets?" Jack flung their coats at the empty bar stool near Violet, before both boys ran toward the billiards table. Their father was right behind them, still wearing his sheriff's uniform. His face was drawn tight, his lips pressed together. He was pissed about something and headed straight for Violet. His sisters immediately stood up, as though they intended to intervene.

Marcus rolled his eyes, shaking his head at their united front. "Now you've got my sisters protecting you?"

"I only need protection from *credible* threats." Violet rose to her feet and stepped between Tessa and Finn. "And you, Sheriff King, are no threat."

Agent Grayson Wyatt, who was assigned to tail Tessa, appeared out of nowhere and asked, "Is everyone okay over here?"

Marcus gave a tense nod but didn't break eye contact with Violet. Her heart thrummed in anticipation of whatever verbal confrontation he'd come to wage. With so many witnesses currently surrounding them, they could engage in a true sparring match and not get sidetracked into another distracting make-out session.

"You know what this party needs?" Aunt Freckles clapped her hands together so hard Violet feared one of the woman's false red fingernails would fly off. She pointed at the jukebox that was playing a fast-tempo George Strait song. "Dancing!"

Freckles, using a surprising amount of strength, shoved Tessa directly into Agent Wyatt's arms. Dahlia, the only single woman safe behind the bar, had the audacity to smile in amusement.

"Finn, you go with Agent Doherty," Freckles continued, and Violet's blood drained from her face because she knew exactly what was coming next. "And Marcus, you and Violet can talk about whatever you need to talk about on the dance floor."

Talking one-on-one with Marcus was the last thing Violet wanted to do. Standing so close to him as he whirled her around a bunch of barroom tables was even less appealing. Unfortunately, though, she was now stuck doing both.

The only alternatives would be to fake an injury, which would worry Jordan, who kept glancing in her direction. Or to refuse, which would be the same thing as admitting that Marcus had any sort of effect on her. There was no way she would give him the satisfaction.

"I thought this was supposed to be a girls' night out," she said when they were finally out of earshot.

"And I thought that you would fight fair," Marcus

replied before spinning her under his arm and deftly pulling her back without missing a step. He was surprisingly more adept at leading her in a fast-paced two-step than he had been during their first waltz at her *quinceañera*.

"First of all, why does everything have to be a fight with you?" Before he could answer, she added, "And who are you to decide what's fair?"

"Okay, so maybe I phrased that wrong," Marcus admitted, his jaw tight. "But you showed up at my office looking hot as hell and maybe I'm a little pissed at myself for thinking things could be different when you kissed me like that."

When her brain finally processed what he said, he was twirling her under his arm again. She ducked her head for a second spin and *accidentally* brought her high heel down on top of his boot. He flinched but didn't stop dancing.

"I didn't kiss *you*. You kissed *me*." Violet forced a smile at Jack and Jordan, who waved to her from the billiards table where they were playing pool with a couple of off-duty Secret Service agents. "And how would one kiss make a difference between us? Did you think it would erase everything else that has happened?"

"That's another thing. We've never even talked about what exactly happened fourteen years ago. Every time it gets brought up, someone interrupts us."

"So is that why you're here?" Violet pivoted on the two count, forcing him to go backward so that she was leading. "You came tearing through those doors all hell-bent on rehashing our past? Because I really don't think *now* is the best time to have that conversation with half of your family as an audience."

"No, I came here because Reed Nakamoto thinks you sweet-talked me into not calling Kendra Broman as a witness."

"The way he tried to sweet-talk Judge Calhoun into extending the preliminary hearing during their impromptu basketball game today? I don't care how many free shots Reed purposely misses, my motion to dismiss has already been filed."

"Was that before or after you made that comment about letting my badge come between us?" Marcus asked, then quickly continued, "Because I might get easily distracted by your kisses, but at the end of the day, I still have a job to do."

"I filed it this morning, and how you do your job really isn't any of my concern. I meant the badge was *literally* coming between us, Marcus. I could feel the points of your star poking into my boob."

Maybe mentioning her breasts was the wrong thing to say right that second, because his eyes dropped to the open lines of her suit jacket where her skin was flushed, rising and falling with each angry breath expanding her rib cage.

He made a growling sound before quickly looking at something off in the distance. The song on the jukebox changed, but he continued to dance, albeit at a slower pace. She should pull away, but deep down

Violet liked the power she had over him. Maybe sub-consciously she *had* been trying to seduce him. She'd certainly thought of it for a split second. But he was also trying to seduce her with the way his forearm locked around her waist and skillfully held her in place against him.

"I have a serious question," Marcus said, as though their conversation up until now hadn't been all that serious. "And it's a little off topic."

Normally, she'd welcome the chance to switch the subject; however, she had a feeling this one wasn't going to be any less antagonistic. Or personal. But she wasn't about to back down now. "Go ahead."

"What do you think your mom is going to do when she finds out you're still here with me?"

"I'm not *with* you. Why would she think that?"

He rolled his eyes. "You know what I mean. The judge issued a gag order, and we've managed to keep things out of the press so far. But eventually the senator is going to find out you're here in Teton Ridge."

"Of course she's going to find out. And it won't be from the press. I'll tell her when I decide it's the right time."

"Will she make you go home to Texas?"

"Marcus, I'm a grown woman. I pay my own bills and make my own decisions. Nobody makes me do anything I don't want to do. Including my mother."

He made a scoffing sound. "I don't know why you're getting so defensive. You have no problem telling me how I should feel about *my* family. Hell, you're being paid to interfere in my relationship with my mom and my brother."

Violet shook her head. "I'm not being paid. I agreed to represent MJ pro bono."

"Oh, come on. My family has more money than they know what to do with, and public defenders are notoriously underpaid." He paused a beat, as though he'd just recalled that her family was nearly as wealthy as his. "So what's in it for you? The chance to get me back for something I never even did?"

"That's cute how you think my being here has anything to do with you," she replied. "I'm simply helping out an old family friend by using my legal expertise and doing what I was trained to do. Pissing you off in the process is just an added bonus."

"What an interesting coincidence that your job involves freeing the very same people who break the laws that my job requires me to enforce."

"Coincidence? Again, you're giving yourself too much credit if you think my career choice had anything to do with you. Unlike you, I hadn't been creeping around on the internet trying to figure out what you did for a living."

"I wasn't creeping." Marcus's expression was so insistent, he looked like his sons when they asked for seconds of dessert. "But speaking of what you do, whatever happened to your dream of becoming a prosecutor?"

"That dream crashed around the same time my dream of becoming a mom was shot down."

"You mean when *we* lost the babies?" His quiet statement caused the righteous air to suddenly whoosh from her lungs.

She quickly recovered, though. "You say *we*, as though both of us went through such a traumatic experience together."

"Physically, no. Obviously, you had it way worse than me, and now I have to live with the fact that I wasn't there for you when you needed me most. But just because I didn't know all the circumstances at the time doesn't mean I didn't suffer a loss." Marcus's eyes seemed to glisten, and his voice grew wobbly but more passionate as he stopped dancing altogether. "Vi, I wanted our babies as much as I once wanted you."

Her knees gave out, and she might've stumbled if he hadn't been holding her so firmly against him. She'd been so hurt by the silence all these years that she'd never really considered the possibility that he would've been equally upset about losing the babies— the ones that he'd apparently wanted. All this time, Violet had assumed he'd been relieved to dodge the young-fatherhood bullet.

No wonder he'd made those earlier comments about her relationship with her mom, considering her mother was the one who'd led him to believe the worst. Violet was pretty damn mad at the woman herself. But like she'd told Marcus earlier, she would deal with her mom in her own way. This wasn't the best time or place to be unpacking all these emotions they'd never fully processed.

Finn and Duke crashed into them as they attempted an ill-fated swing lift. When had the song changed to a fast-paced one again? And when had Duke come back inside the bar?

Violet quickly glanced around the room to see if anyone had been watching their tense exchange. Yep. Several pairs of eyes were, in fact, on them. Including Jack's and Jordan's. She cleared her throat and stepped out of his arms. "I think that should be enough dancing to satisfy Aunt Freckles. I'm going to go finish my wine."

And maybe a shot of something stronger.

For the millionth time that week, Violet silently cursed herself for not leaving Teton Ridge when she'd had a chance. She liked it better when she didn't have to think about running into Marcus King on a daily basis.

Chapter Seven

Marcus's pain-filled words were still playing in Violet's head later that following week as she set up a temporary workstation inside the unused pool house at the Twin Kings. Not that MJ's case required that much time or effort since they were still in the pre-trial stage. Normally, Violet managed several ongoing cases at once, and most of them involved much bigger charges and stakes. But since she'd taken a personal leave of absence from her job to handle MJ's case, she had to be in constant communication with the other attorneys in her office who were covering the clients on her caseload.

Tessa had claimed her father's old study for research, and Sherilee had set up some sort of public-relations headquarters in the west wing of the house. So that left the glass-enclosed pool house that wasn't in use during the winter months. The temporary office smelled faintly of chlorine and sunscreen yet had a massive custom-built river-rock fireplace taking up an entire wall. The design was intended to be used during the seasons when the weather allowed for outdoor entertaining, but it worked well for keeping the place heated now that they were well into February.

Violet moved a few pool noodles off a chaise lounge and fired up her laptop. Of course, the first email she responded to required her to type the word *once* and she immediately lost her train of thought.

Once.

I wanted our babies as much as I once wanted you.

That's what Marcus had said to her when they'd been dancing. Clearly, he didn't want her anymore. Not that she wanted him. Obviously. But it'd be nice if they could at least get along.

She'd thought they'd turned a corner that night at Big Millie's when he'd let his guard down and opened up about losing the babies. But then the following day, she'd run into him at Burnworth's Bakery and he'd pretended he didn't even know her. In fact, several times last week she'd seen him on duty patrolling the small town of Teton Ridge, and the most he'd been able to manage was a brief nod in her direction.

It was almost as though he didn't want anyone in

town seeing them being even slightly friendly toward each other.

Then, last Sunday, she'd gone out for a run on one of the many trails crisscrossing the vast ranch and saw him and the twins riding their bikes toward the main house. The boys were excited to see her and Jordan immediately wanted to know if she wanted a tour of their "brand-new" cabin.

"Well, it's not real brand-new," Jack clarified. "We used to live there before when our mom was alive, but me and Jordan don't remember that from way back when. But we have a Nintendo Switch and you can play the red controller if you want. It has motion controls and rumbles in your hands so you can feel when you go over the bumpy track."

Violet had tried not to blink too much at the casual mention of their mom in passing. "I think I may have to brush up on my video game skills before I take on the responsibility of the red controller. Maybe some other time?"

Marcus had let out the breath he'd been holding, looking visibly relieved. "Speaking of added features." He nodded at her smartphone on the elastic holder around her bicep. "How's your GPS reception on that thing? The open pastures on the west side of the ranch make it hard to get lost. But the trails on this side are way narrower and confusing for people who didn't grow up here."

"Well, maybe you'll get lucky, and I'll wind up lost," she'd retorted. He hadn't cared about her safety or her sense of direction all last week when he'd ignored her in town. Yet now he suddenly felt the need to patronize her with his knowledge of the rugged tree-lined terrain.

So now that she'd set up an office in the pool house and wasn't in town at the law library as much, she was making more of an effort to be the one who ignored him. Violet responded to several emails and had a video conference with one of her clients turned state's witness housed in protective custody at the West Tower Detention Facility. When she ran out of tasks, she returned to the main house to find out Sherilee had insisted Marcus and the twins come for a family meal that night.

The twins, as usual, had been excited to see Violet, regaling her with stories about their school day. Their father, as usual, was much harder to read. Marcus's family might be a little pushy, but nobody was forcing him to be here. She had to give him credit for at least making the attempt to keep things as normal as he could for his children.

As they took their places in the dining room, Violet watched Marcus reach across the table to help Jack pour his lemonade into one of the fancy crystal goblets Sherilee insisted everyone use. Then he silently helped Jordan spread the cold pat of butter across his crumbling biscuit. Violet wondered if he would've been as gentle and loving as a father to her twins, had they survived.

Guilt caused her chest to tighten. Of course he

would have been. The man was born to be an amazing dad. It was his role as ex-boyfriend and big brother that could use a little work.

"You have any plans this weekend, MJ?" Freckles asked.

"No!" both Marcus and his mother said in unison.

MJ threw his napkin on the table. "So I'm a prisoner in my own home now?"

Sherilee returned MJ's napkin to him as if he'd accidentally misplaced it. "I thought we agreed that you'd keep a low profile and not leave the ranch until things calm down."

"You mean you and Sheriff Trust-No-One over there agreed," MJ replied, displaying his most angst-filled teenaged glare in Marcus's direction.

"I'm pretty sure your defense attorney would recommend the same thing." Great, now Marcus was drawing Violet into their petty squabble.

Violet took a sip of her ice water, wishing she hadn't declined the predinner cocktail hour, before speaking directly to MJ. "Only because I think the judge would look more favorably on you not drawing any attention to yourself by leaving the ranch. Unless, of course, you were going to a job or a college class, perhaps."

"Yeah, well, I don't have a job. And I'm not going to college," MJ announced, making his mom gasp. He looked Sherilee in the eye and added, "Ever."

"I can give you a job," Uncle Rider offered. "Plenty of stalls need mucking."

"So my only choices are house arrest and forced labor. I'd probably have it better in prison."

Violet's left eye twitched. She thought about the client she'd just spoken with via video chat. The woman had been in and out of institutions since she was twelve years old and was facing ten more years if she didn't cooperate with prosecutors to implicate her pimp as the head of a human-trafficking ring.

The young man sitting before her had no idea what a real prison smelled like, let alone felt like. MJ's pessimistic attitude—while understandable— was probably the biggest contributor to his current predicament. He was young, privileged and way too sheltered to have such a big chip on his shoulder. He was also drifting through life aimlessly with no goals and way too much free time on his hands, which only gave him more opportunity to stew.

"Peyton's mom's boyfriend was in prison," young Amelia said. "She went to visit him every month, and there was a big, mean dog that sniffed her mom to make sure she didn't sneak any keys or bad stuff into him."

"Really?" Dahlia tilted her head at her daughter. "Peyton's mom told me that her boyfriend lived in Montana."

"They have prisons in Montana," Rider said. "Got an old rodeo buddy who did a dime in the state pen back in the seventies. Said it was the worst stretch he's ever done. But he did meet his wife there. She was a guard. So I guess it worked out for him."

"Anyone else see a problem with the direction of this conversation?" Duke nodded subtly at the wide-eyed expressions on his nephews' faces. "Maybe we should change the subject to something that is a little less *Shawshank Redemption*."

"So if I can't leave," MJ said returning the topic back to himself, "can I at least have some friends over to hang out?"

"Like who?" Sherilee might've lifted a sculpted brow if her Botoxed forehead would've allowed it.

MJ shrugged. "Like Kendra?"

"No!" Marcus and Sherilee said in unison. Again.

MJ turned pleading eyes toward Violet, who seemed to be his only ally at the table. Or at least the only person legally contracted to represent him. She sighed. "I don't see a problem with Kendra visiting as long as you guys are properly chaperoned and only engaging in activities suitable for teenagers."

Finn plopped another spoonful of chicken and dumplings on her plate. "Violet, you might need to define what your expectations of a suitable activity is."

"I don't know. What do eighteen-year-olds do for fun nowadays?"

"The same thing *we* used to do when we were that age." Marcus stared expectantly at her, and Violet's face felt as though it was going to catch on fire.

Sherilee choked on her wine, while Freckles and Finn giggled like schoolgirls.

"In that case, count me out as a chaperone." Duke

sat back in his chair and rubbed his flat stomach. "Mom and Dad used to make me tag along with Vi and Marcus to keep an eye on them, but I always ended up getting ditched."

"Why would they ditch you, Uncle Duke?" Jordan wanted to know. "You're the funnest one in the family, and you're real good at playing football and Uno and video games."

"Because back then, your dad and Miss Violet preferred to play a two-person game called—"

"Twister," Violet interrupted Duke just in time, which made Finn and Freckles giggle even more. Even Dahlia had to cover her mouth to keep from laughing.

Duke held up his hands innocently. "Hey, I was going to say Battleship. But that might be a better description for the game you two are *currently* playing."

Marcus narrowed his eyes at his brother but didn't dispute the fact that he and Violet were, in fact, acting like adversaries who wanted to sink each other.

"Yeah, we get it. Marcus and Violet hate each other," MJ said, causing Jordan to gasp with concern. "But can we focus on me and my situation for a second?"

"It's okay," Marcus said softly as he patted his son's shoulder. "Violet and I are old friends who just squabble sometimes. We don't really hate each other."

Jack's eyes sought Violet's across the table, and

she nodded in confirmation. At least she could reassure the boys, even if she couldn't reassure herself.

MJ, though, continued, "You guys can't keep me and Kendra away from each other forever."

Rider wiped some sauce off his bushy mustache. "I think your girlfriend's dad might have something to say about that. Or did you forget that you sucker punched her old man?"

"I apologized. Besides, it's not my fault Deputy Broman hates our family. At some point, he's gonna have to get over it because I love his daughter and eventually we'll find a way to be together no matter what. We're like Romeo and Juliet."

"Did you ever actually rèad *Romeo and Juliet*?" Marcus asked.

"I read most of it. We had to do a book report on it my sophomore year."

Violet felt another migraine coming on and pinched the bridge of her nose. In an effort to present her client in the most favorable light in court, she'd gone through MJ's high-school transcripts and was disappointed to see so many below-average grades and comments from his teachers about how smart he was but how rarely he turned in assignments.

"Yeah, well, if you'd ever finished something you'd started, you'd know that things don't work out too well for that particular pair of star-crossed lovers." Marcus tilted back the rest of his beer and swallowed before adding, "In fact, it rarely does."

Whoa. That second dig was definitely directed at

her. Forgetting her earlier reassurance to Jordan and Jack about not hating their father, Violet narrowed her eyes at Marcus. "Do we really need all your extra judgments thrown in for dramatic flair?"

"What extra judgments?"

"Oh, you know, the dig about MJ not finishing what he starts. Then the bonus commentary about young love rarely working out."

He held up his open palms. "I was merely stating the facts. Romeo and Juliet were in love, and it didn't end so well. I'm sorry if that hits a little too close to home for you, Violet."

"Well, if we're going to state *facts*, then let's talk about how Romeo totally overreacted. If he had just been patient and thought things through instead of jumping to conclusions, Juliet would've gotten up and explained everything. But your boy had to act all rash and assume the worst and turn the whole thing into a tragedy."

"How do you know Romeo wasn't also dealing with Juliet's mom planting seeds of doubt in his head?" Marcus argued. "Telling him that her daughter was better off without him?"

"If that was the case, then he should've realized her mom didn't want them to be together in the first place," Violet countered. "The seeds of doubt should never have taken root."

"All I'm saying is that it might've been nice if she'd written him a note or something letting him know what was going on."

"She *did* write a note. How was she to know that he never got it?"

"Wait. Are we still talking about Romeo and Juliet?" Rider asked. "Freckles made me watch the movie once, but I fell asleep before it got to all of that."

"Yeah, this story sounds boring," Jack said while trying to balance his spoon on his nose. "Is it time for dessert yet?"

And just like that, Freckles retreated to the kitchen to serve up the banana cream pie to the kids. Sherilee followed to make sure her sister-in-law was only using the dairy-free whipped topping instead of real cream.

Apparently, nobody else wanted to listen to Marcus and Violet rehash the story of their breakup using euphemisms from a literary classic, either. The entire King family jumped at the chance to clear out of the dining room without bothering to make a single excuse for their abrupt exits.

Violet and Marcus remained in their seats across the table from each other, the tension between them having been stretched to their limits, but now sagging. Like a deflated party balloon.

"We never used to fight like this before." Marcus finally broke the silence. "It doesn't feel right to be at odds this way. But at the same time, I can't stop myself from getting sucked into even the slightest argument. I'm really sorry, Violet. I don't know what the hell I'm doing."

"Do you remember the first time you asked me out?" she shifted forward in her seat.

He tilted his head at her before staring up at the ceiling for several seconds. Finally, he shook his head. "I remember going to the movies a handful of times, and playing mini golf, and driving to Six Flags when we tried to set Duke up with your roommate from boarding school and he came out to us before we got on the first roller coaster. Oh, and that one time you talked me into taking you to the Justin Timberlake concert and caught me singing along to all the lyrics I pretended I didn't know. But I can't think of the first time."

"That's because you never did ask me out, Marcus. It just sort of happened, like it was a given that we were together. We never really had to work at having a relationship before." She sighed. "Every time I look at you, I see the boy you used to be. I mean, in a more manly body, but it's still you. Except it's not, because you're so different now. We both are so much more cynical, for good reason, which means being around you isn't as natural as it used to be. The problem is that my brain doesn't want to accept that, so my tongue lashes out."

His chest expanded, and even from a distance she could see his pupils dilate. "Maybe your tongue needs something else to keep it occupied?"

Adrenaline spiked through Violet, causing her to briefly calculate whether it would be faster to walk around the table or to just hurdle over the draped white linen tablecloth and crystal goblets to get into his arms.

Luckily, the sudden appearance of Jack and Jordan carrying two plates of pie into the dining room saved her from doing something she'd later regret.

Having been both an eighteen-year-old virgin and now a thirty-two-year-old experienced man, Marcus had never wanted a woman more than he wanted Violet Cortez-Hill. He was no longer an impulsive youth, though, and knew full well the potential consequences of allowing history to repeat itself.

Not that Marcus wanted to go down that road again. Especially not after the unwarranted lecture he'd gotten from Reed Nakamoto about not letting Violet sweet-talk him into anything. He'd purposely stayed away from her every time he'd seen her in town, just so that nobody could say something was going on between them.

Still, it was getting awfully hard to avoid the woman when they were living on the same damn ranch. Especially when his sons loved seeing her so often and his mom kept insisting on her torturous and chaotic family dinners. Plus, deep down, he didn't really want to avoid her. He wanted to go back to how things used to be. But that would never happen until they got everything off their chests.

On his way home from work Tuesday, he was driving past the main house and saw Violet walking from the stables in the direction of the pool house.

The kids had told him all about her new office space and how they'd helped her decorate with their home-made art and trail finds. Oh, and some colorful beach towels to make her feel like she was back in sunny Texas. It sounded like she was already homesick.

Violet waved, so he slowed the cruiser and asked, "Have you seen the boys? My mom picked them up from school, but she isn't answering her cell phone."

"Mrs. King said she had some sort of meeting with Special Agent in Charge Simon in the conference room attached to the agents' bunkhouse. She asked me to watch the twins for a few minutes, and they wanted me to see their new horses."

Marcus put the SUV in Park and climbed out. "So they're in the stables?"

"Well, they were. But then Uncle Rider offered to take them out on the trail. I hope you don't mind that I didn't go with them, but I didn't have any suitable shoes or riding clothes, so I decided to stay back."

He glanced at her fitted black pants and suede fashion boots with the fur trim. Nobody was going to confuse her for a cattle hand, but he'd seen people climb into the saddle wearing a lot worse. Then a memory clicked into place. One of him taking a sixteen-year-old Violet out on her first ride. Marcus had stupidly wanted to show off one of their prime stallions, a young, spirited buck who, unfortunately, attempted to mount Violet's mare. While she was riding her.

But that was so long ago. Plus, she'd gone to

an elite boarding school in Virginia with a world-famous equestrian program. Surely she couldn't be…

"Wait. Are you still afraid of horses?"

"I'm not *afraid* of them," she said, then lowered her voice as a gelding in the outside corral passed by. "It's just that they don't really like me all that much."

"How can an animal not like you?"

"I don't know. Maybe they sense my nervousness."

Marcus bit back a grin. "Have you ever gotten back in the saddle again?"

"Of course. When I was in college, I decided to conquer my fear once and for all. It was spring break, and a group of us went to Cancún. The resort had horseback riding on the beach, so I figured having a change of scenery wouldn't trigger my traumatic memory of that awkward day with Fabio."

Marcus winced. "Yeah, the name of the horse should've been my first clue that he wasn't ready for a leisurely trail ride."

"If it's any consolation, I chose a small, unassuming-looking horse named Gidget the second time around and she wasn't much better." Violet must've seen the confusion on his face because she held up a hand. "No, she didn't try to mount anything. She just thought she was a surfer and kept rushing into the waves and rolling around in the sand. Again with me on her back. So suffice it to say that horses are one of the few creatures who refuse to acknowledge my commanding presence."

Marcus allowed his eyes to wander down the snug fabric encasing her long legs. Violet certainly had a commanding presence that was becoming increasingly more difficult for him *not* to acknowledge.

"You know, Fabio's still here. He's an old man now and sired so many colts, we had to finally retire him. He's over in Shady Acres." Marcus put his arm over her shoulders to steer her away from the outer corrals. "Come on. I'll take you to see him, and you'll realize that he's not so threatening anymore."

"Shady Acres?" Violet angled her head sideways as she questioned him, but she didn't pull away.

"Yeah. You know, from the TV show *Golden Girls*? Finn loves to name the horses and the different wings of the stables after her favorite sitcoms. If I remember correctly, the horse you were riding that day was also named after a character in that show. Blanche. Which explains why Fabio couldn't stay away from her."

Violet let out a full-bodied laugh, and Marcus instinctively pulled her in tighter. This. This is what it used to feel like between them. They would playfully tease and crack jokes and walk completely in step with each other. Violet fit perfectly beside him.

In fact, he was tempted to take her the long way around the stables just so they could keep walking like this. But Finn had carved wooden signs above each row of stalls, and Rider believed in putting the older horses front and center so that nobody forgot how hard they'd once worked for the ranch. So Shady

Acres was the first section they came across, and Fabio was in the third stall down.

"No way," Violet said when she saw the once-palomino-colored muzzle was speckled with gray. "This can't be him. What happened to his flowing golden mane?"

"Let's just say that, nowadays, he likes his food much more than he likes the ladies. He managed to get his head stuck in one of those self-feeding hay nets. His mane was all tangled up in the netting, so we had to buzz it off. It hasn't grown back yet."

"He certainly looks way less threatening now. Don't you, boy?"

"Here." Marcus pulled an apple-flavored oat biscuit out of his inside jacket pocket. "Give him this, and he will love you forever."

Violet wrinkled her nose. "You keep horse treats in your uniform pocket?"

"I'm a sheriff in a small ranching town. Half of my job consists of interacting with citizens who are either riding livestock, herding livestock or complaining about someone else's livestock. I've got dog treats in the other pocket. Now, hold your fingers out straight like this."

Violet's palm was stiff when he handed her the biscuit, and Marcus slid his hand under hers to coax her into relaxing. A zing of awareness shot through him at the feel of her warm skin. She must've felt it, too, because she shuddered delicately. Or maybe she was afraid of Fabio's protruding teeth coming her way.

"It's okay. Just hold yourself steady." Standing behind her, Marcus put his other hand on her waist so she'd know he was right there with her to intervene in case something happened.

But as expected, Fabio took the treat, smacked his lips as he chewed, then snorted in appreciation. Violet's body relaxed against Marcus, and he let his fingers splay around the curve above her hip, his thumb grazing along the soft, stretchy fabric toward her waistband.

"That wasn't so bad." She sighed, and it took him a second to realize she was talking about the horse.

Or maybe she wasn't.

The back of her neck was resting against his shoulder, so when she tilted her face to look at him, her smiling lips were inches from his. Marcus groaned before claiming her mouth with his own.

Unlike two weeks ago in his office, though, this kiss started out tentative and slow. As if neither one wanted to be the first to lose control.

But as their tongues explored deeper, his fingers followed suit, and soon his hand was nudging under the hem of her sweater. Violet gave a breathless moan and twisted so that she could face him, which only pressed their bodies closer together.

The unmistakable whirling of an engine sounded outside, and Violet pulled away slightly. Her breath was warm, and her voice was raspy as she whispered, "Is that the helicopter?"

"Probably." He moved his lips to her cheek and pressed light kisses along her jawline. After a daring paparazzo had chartered a local sight-seeing chopper to get some long-range aerial photos of Tessa, the Secret Service agents had been doing routine air patrols around the ranch twice a day.

When his mouth dipped lower to her neck, she threw her head back and moaned. Her fingers were stroking underneath the lined collar of his jacket, holding his head in place as she gave him full access to the tender spot where her pulse was beating out a frenzied tempo. Marcus was so intent on what he was doing, he barely heard her whisper, "What if someone catches us?"

"Come on, we can go in here." Marcus had noticed that the stall across from Fabio's was empty, and he pulled her inside. He rolled the solid wood sliding door closed, but that only hid them from the chest down. There was a pile of straw in one corner that looked clean, and he steered her in that direction. "We're going to have to hunker down if we want to stay out of sight."

Violet's laugh was low and throaty as she sank into the pile as though it was a regal throne. "This reminds me of the time our families were both staying at Camp David for that Department of Defense conference, and we snuck out of our cabins and hid in the archery shed. Except you're a much better kisser now."

"That's because I remembered to take out my retainer this time." Marcus lowered himself over her, determined to prove how much better he was at everything. She eagerly embraced him, lifting her arms around his neck and pulling him closer. Her sweater rose, and he slid both of his palms higher, caressing the silky warmth of her bare skin until his hands were just below her breasts.

They were lying side by side, facing each other, and his arousal strained against his uniform pants as she pressed herself against him. Without breaking their kiss, Violet's fingers began to work at the heavy clasp of his leather duty belt.

But before she could get it undone, they heard voices entering the stables. Violet's eyes flew open, and she put a finger to her lips, as if Marcus needed the warning to stay quiet. He was rock hard, and there was straw sticking out of Violet's hair at all angles. Anyone who saw them would know exactly what they'd been up to.

The voices—at least three of them—grew closer. Violet whispered into his ear, "Do you think you can shift your weight back the other direction? Your gun is digging into my hip."

He responded through clenched teeth. "If I shift back to where I just was, it won't be my gun pressing into you."

Squeezing her eyes shut, she reminded him of

Jack when he was a toddler and thought that if he couldn't see anyone around him, then nobody could see him, either. Marcus used his elbows to lift his torso enough to roll away but then froze at the rustling sound of the straw surrounding them.

"Shhh," she said. He didn't think it would be possible to make her blush more than she already was, but then he realized the rosy color spreading up her neck wasn't from embarrassment. It was whisker burn.

The voices were now right outside their row of stalls. He recognized the annoyance in his sister Tessa's tone before realizing who she was talking to. He slowly shifted to his knees so he could see out one of the slats.

Congressman Davis Townsend, better known as Congressman Smooth to the rest of their family members. Nobody understood what Tessa saw in the up-and-coming politician, who was clearly using her to get closer to the famous King name.

From the sound of things, the congressman was upset about all the media hype surrounding Tessa and Agent Wyatt, who was now standing by quietly as Tessa rejected Townsend's not-so-romantic proposal. Suddenly, the conversation turned angry.

"Together, we could've gone further than Roper King could ever have hoped," Townsend said, and Marcus's blood rang in his ears. Nobody was going to disrespect his dead father on the very ranch that his legacy had been built upon.

Marcus started to rise, but Violet tugged on his hand. Her whisper was hushed yet firm. "Let your sister handle this, Marcus. She's been bottling everything in lately and needs to speak her piece."

As if to prove Violet right, Tessa finally snapped. "My dad got exactly as far as he wanted, Davis. And, for the record, he hated people who needed to use someone else to get ahead."

"I was never using you. At least, not any more than you were using me."

"How did I use you?" his sister asked. She was a political analyst with a prime-time show interviewing some of the most powerful world leaders. At least she was finally acting like herself again. "I'd love to hear this."

"Tessa King had the reputation of being a cold, cutthroat bitch before I came along. I humanized you. Being in a relationship with me made you at least seem like a real woman."

Marcus was on his knees and ready to spring into action, his fists clenching at the insult to his sister. He didn't think he could stay silent much longer.

"I think you need to leave now, Congressman Townsend," Tessa said.

"But your mother invited me—"

"Miss King has politely asked you to leave," Agent Wyatt interrupted in a direct, deliberate voice. "I'll have the command center radio your pilot so you can fly out of here on your own accord."

"Or else what?" Davis's chin lifted.

Oh, hell no.

Wyatt was more than trained to handle the situation on his own, but Marcus was a law-enforcement officer as much as he was a brother. Challenging a sitting member of the House of Representatives would be a risky career move for the agent, who'd already gone above and beyond his duty keeping Tessa safe.

Plus, Marcus was not about to let some sanctimonious prick stay on his family's property a second longer. He was out of the stall before Violet could pull him back.

It took every ounce of training for Marcus to keep himself reined in as he purposefully approached the congressman. "Or else we can escort you from the premises in the back of the Ridgecrest County Sheriff's unit."

She should've stayed put, but Violet stepped to his side, risking her own reputation by backing him up. Marcus's chest swelled with pride and appreciation.

Three pairs of eyes darted back and forth between them. Instead of giving anyone the chance to question what he and Violet were doing there in the first place, Marcus continued, "Before you make your choice, it's only fair to warn you that the back seat of my squad car doesn't have tinted windows. I'm sure the press stationed outside the gates would love to get a great shot of you back there."

Townsend took a step back in retreat and flashed

his ridiculous fake grin. "We're good. I was just leaving."

The congressman turned to go, and Marcus followed to make sure the man actually left the premises, not just the stables. Violet kept up with Marcus's determined strides, and right before they exited into the daylight, she slipped her palm into his, gave his hand a firm squeeze and then dropped her arm to her side before they went outside.

He wished he could've glanced in her direction to see what she was thinking, but he had to keep his eyes trained on the back of Townsend's head.

Initially, he thought the hand squeeze was a silent promise to finish what they'd started back in the horse stall. But then, in his peripheral vision, he spotted his sons and Uncle Rider cooling down their horses in the outer corral.

More than likely, she was simply giving him the warning that they now had an audience. Playtime was over, and they were back to being adversaries.

Chapter Eight

Violet finished her list of exhibits for the pretrial hearing and closed her laptop before deciding to take a long run to clear her brain. She'd tried to put Marcus out of her mind for the past few days but couldn't stop thinking about how close they'd actually come to both literally and figuratively having a roll in the hay.

She especially couldn't stop thinking about how his initial response had been to protect Tessa during his sister's argument with her ex-boyfriend. Even with emotions running high, Marcus had been extremely professional in the way he'd handled the trespassing congressman, considering the fact that Violet herself had wanted to punch the jerk.

Marcus truly did have his family's best interests at heart, and it was becoming increasingly apparent that he just wanted to protect his siblings. All of them. Including MJ. Now if she could only convince him that the way he was going about looking out for his brother would surely backfire.

She passed an old tree with a faded carving in its trunk along with an arrow. *RKx2 was here.* Finn had explained to Violet that as boys, their father and Uncle Rider used to carry pocketknives and scratch their initials into trees along their favorite trails so that they would know where they'd already explored.

"*RKx2* is a lot shorter to write than spelling out *Rider King and Roper King* every time," Finn had said. "If you follow the arrows below the initials, they'll always point you toward the stables so you can't get lost. They were adults, though, when they purchased the western acres. So if you ever end up on that side of the ranch, you better have a GPS because there aren't any RKx2 markers over there."

Every time Violet went for a run, she always tried to follow the marked trees on the east side, since it gave her a better sense of direction. However, seeing the carving today gave her an unexpected sense of comfort, as well. Marcus's father had been one of the smartest and most diplomatic men she'd ever known. Sure, he was a politician and could smooth talk with the best of them. Yet, he always knew the right thing to say and exactly when to say it.

"Hey, Mr. King, if you're up there listening,

maybe you could give me the right words to talk to your oldest son." She felt silly making the request aloud. Mostly because her job was to come up with convincing arguments. So she added, "Preferably at a time when he's willing to actually listen."

She was only a mile into her run when she passed the small road leading to the family cemetery and saw Marcus's patrol vehicle parked at the top. Her heart skipped several beats. She hadn't expected the opportunity to talk to the man to pop up this soon.

Violet paused, jogging in place. She shouldn't interrupt him while he was visiting his father's grave. But then again, she *had* asked Roper King himself for a sign. What should she say, though?

After arguing with herself for several minutes, she finally decided to continue her run, taking the two-mile loop path skirting a cluster of trees. She told herself that if Marcus was still there when she returned this way, then she would approach him.

Violet wasn't the fastest runner to begin with, and despite slowing her pace, his vehicle was still there when she finally made it back to the crossroad. Ugh. Even though she'd yet to come up with the right words, she was going to have to say something. Otherwise, she'd regret wasting the opportunity and then spend the rest of the day kicking herself for not having the courage.

And Violet didn't want any more regrets when it came to Marcus King.

Rolling her shoulders a few times before walking through the gated path, she expected to find him standing in front of the newest—and biggest—granite headstone in the cemetery. When she realized he was standing in front of his wife's headstone, though, Violet froze before trying to quietly backtrack her steps.

Unfortunately, Marcus had already turned his head and spotted her.

She lifted her hand in a wave before realizing that maybe that wasn't the most appropriate greeting under the circumstances. "I didn't want to interrupt you. I was just hoping to catch you…" *Not* alone. *Don't say alone.* "I should've waited until you were done with your visit."

"I was pretty much done." Marcus rocked back on his boot heels. "What's up?"

Violet should've brought up the subject of MJ, but instead said the first thing that popped into her head. "Tell me about her."

Judging from the surprised expression that crossed his face, he clearly hadn't been expecting her to say that. "About Brie?"

Damn it. Maybe that was out of bounds. "I mean, only if it's not weird."

"Everything has been weird since you arrived, Vi. So why would we want to go back to normal now?" Marcus let out a deep breath and shoved his hands in his pockets. "I might as well tell you all about her since she knew all about you."

Now it was her turn to be surprised. "You talked to your wife about me?"

"Yeah. I used to talk to her about everything. I mean, not initially. We'd gone to high school together but never really hung out back then. According to her, she had a crush on me, but everyone knew I was in love with someone else who lived far away." Marcus obviously meant Violet, but she didn't want to make this conversation about her, so she nodded, and he continued, "I was a mess after I got out of boot camp. I had a one-week leave before starting my advanced individual training school, so I came back to the ranch to get over…whatever had gone wrong between us. Duke was playing in some garage band back then with Dahlia's ex-husband and talked me into coming to one of their gigs. Brie was there, and she came over to say hi. I ended up crying in my beer the whole night and telling her all about us. Or at least the version of us that I knew at the time."

Violet didn't like the feeling of jealousy blossoming inside her. Not because Marcus had shared the details of their relationship with another woman, but because Violet hadn't been able to do the same. Her mother had insisted that they needed to keep the whole thing quiet so that it didn't affect her senate reelection bid. The only other person who'd known was her dad, but he had a tendency to revert to baseball jargon during emotionally vulnerable moments. And nobody wanted to hear "Sometimes you hit a few foul balls before you get that grand slam" after a bad breakup.

Marcus rubbed the back of his neck as he continued, "Brie asked if I wanted to keep in contact while I was at AIT and assured me that she wasn't interested in some sort of rebound fling. I guess she thought I seemed like I could use a friend. Mostly we just followed each other on social media and would text every once in a while. Then, when I went on deployment, she started sending me care packages and little notes and funny cards. I never really stopped thinking about you, but talking to Brie helped keep my mind off what I'd lost. When my four years was up, I came back to Wyoming. I didn't think I'd ever be able to fall in love again after you, but she won me over. Being with her just seemed...easy."

Of course it was easy. Brie didn't have a famous mother trying to keep them physically and emotionally separated. Violet glanced at the headstone, then asked, "Do the twins get to see her family often?"

"Actually, she was raised by her grandparents. Her grandma passed away right after high school, and her grandpa moved into an assisted-living place out in Cheyenne before we started dating."

"Oh, that must've been hard for her. To feel so alone at such a young age."

Marcus nodded. "Probably, but Brie never showed it. She was one of those glass-half-full kind of people. Always had a smile on her face, never said anything bad about anyone. My mom joked that she would've been the perfect politician's wife, but Brie never had those kinds of ambitions. Which was good, because

I didn't, either. She seemed happy being married to a small-town cop and loved being a mom."

Violet heard the quiet part out loud. Brie didn't bring along the baggage of an interfering family. Unlike Violet, who had a controlling mother and who—in Marcus's mind at the time—had chosen her career over their children.

He'd fallen in love with Violet's exact opposite. She'd seen a few framed pictures of Brie and Marcus back at the main house, and even appearance wise, the women had completely different coloring and dressed very differently. A shiver of rejection made its way down Violet's spine.

"I really am sorry for your loss, Marcus. That must've been so hard on you and the boys." She bit her lip. "They must really miss their mom."

His jaw was rigid as he gave a stiff nod.

"And again, I'm sorry for interrupting your visit."

"More like a therapy session." He lifted his face to the sun before shrugging. "I'd been avoiding this place for years before my dad died. In fact, I was dreading his funeral for this very reason. I hated the reminder of what I'd lost. What my sons had lost. But that day at the graveside service, I saw her headstone without so much as a flower on it, and it made me realize that I shouldn't have allowed my hurt to keep me away. Since you've gotten here… I don't know how to explain it, but it just felt like I should be filling her in on everything going on. The boys, MJ, you. She was a good wife and mother, but more than anything else, she was always a great listener. A great partner."

Violet inhaled deeply, unsure of this raw emotion gnawing at something inside of her. It wasn't quite jealousy, despite the fact that she clearly would never be able to fill Brie's shoes when it came to being a loving mother or a doting wife—not that anyone was trying to compete with the memory of a dead woman. Nor was it the implication that Violet's sudden appearance had reopened all of Marcus's old wounds and talking to Brie was again the one thing that seemed to bring him any sort of comfort.

Rather, hearing about Marcus's wife and how much he'd loved her made Violet feel more remorse than anything else. Like she was causing him to be disloyal in some way to Brie. She never would have kissed him knowing he wasn't ready to move on.

She glanced at the freshly turned earth of Roper King's gravesite. There were two flower arrangements which were too fresh to have been leftover from the funeral weeks ago. There was also a collection of little trinkets lined up along the granite ledge, such as a set of gold pilot wings, a thirty-year sobriety chip and a small US flag in a weighted stand.

But the item that caught her attention was a freshly cut log leaning against the headstone with *RKx2* carved into the bark. Perhaps Rider had simply stopped by to visit his brother. Or maybe it was another sign from Marcus's father. It didn't matter, though. There was no way she was going to talk to him about MJ right now. In fact, maybe she'd misread the earlier signs, and Roper King was actually trying to tell her to return to the main house and give his son space.

"Can I give you a ride back down the hill?" Marcus asked.

"No, thanks." She forced a polite smile. "I still need to finish my run."

Marcus had his own demons and hardships he needed to face without her chiming in with her two cents every time they disagreed. It was becoming increasingly clear that it wasn't Violet's place to be his voice of reason. She'd forfeited that opportunity to another woman long ago.

"You're not staying for dinner?" Aunt Freckles asked Marcus the following Friday evening when he dropped off the twins at the main house for the weekly meal that was becoming a bit too frequent. It was also a bit too tension-filled—even by King standards—now that peacekeeping Duke had returned to duty on his aircraft carrier.

"Nah. I'm covering a shift for one of my deputies who needed the night off."

"What a coincidence." Freckles pursed her coral-painted lips. "Violet won't be here for dinner, either."

"Where's she going?" Marcus asked more suspiciously than he'd intended.

"I didn't ask, seeing as how she's a grown woman

and it's not my business." Freckles challenged Marcus with an impish grin.

"Is that your way of telling me that it's not my business, either?"

"Of course it's his business," Sherilee King said sarcastically as she came striding into the kitchen. "Didn't you hear, Freckles? My son is the sheriff of the whole entire county and thinks he's in charge of everything and everyone in his jurisdiction."

Marcus didn't give his mother the satisfaction of rolling his eyes. He was not going to engage in the same old argument that neither of them would win.

"Now, Sherilee, don't give the boy such a hard time for doing his job."

"Thank you, Aunt Freckles." Finally someone was on his side.

But before he could relish in his triumph, Freckles pointed an oven mitt in his direction. "And *you* don't give your mama a hard time for doing *her* job and protecting her babies."

"You mean *baby*, singular," Marcus corrected. "Only one of her young cubs is getting the full mama-bear protection, and it certainly isn't me."

"Oh, I'm protecting you, Marcus." His mother reached for the hunk of cheddar Freckles had been shredding for her baked macaroni and cheese casserole. His mom only ate dairy products when she was stressed. Or when she was annoyed. Or when she thought no one was watching. She chewed before adding, "You're just too stubborn to see it."

"You're protecting me?" Marcus snorted. "How? By undermining my job and my role in the community? Or by installing my ex-girlfriend in our family home to argue with me at every turn?"

"You think I'm enjoying all the increased tension around here?" His mom slapped a manicured hand on the counter. "Every time I turn around, you're squabbling with Violet, or Freckles is bickering with Rider. Even my sweet Duke was getting testy on some secret phone call before he left. And then there's troublemaking Finn egging everyone on like she's an announcer at the state rodeo. My husband— the love of my life—just died, yet my home is filled with so much damn chaos and shouting I can't even hear myself think."

"You eat any more of my cheese, Sherilee, and you're going to have plenty of time alone to think. In the bathroom." Freckles took the wedge of decimated cheddar away from her sister-in-law. "Besides, Rider and I don't bicker. We engage in verbal wrestling, which isn't nearly as fun as our mattress wrestling—"

"Really, Freckles?" His mom thankfully interrupted his aunt. "Do you have to be so graphic *all* the time?"

"Stop being such a prude, Sher. You have six kids, so it's not like you didn't have a little fun in your marriage, too."

"Yeah, but I'm not going around bragging about it to the whole damn world."

"Give it a rest, you two!" Marcus suddenly went from defending himself to refereeing a forty-year dispute between the biggest verbal combatants in the entire King family. He lifted his brow at his mother. "And you accuse everyone else of arguing?"

"This isn't an argument," his mom countered. "This is a discussion. Right, Freckles?"

"Yep. Just a little conversation to clear the air."

"Oh, so now you guys decide to agree?" This time, Marcus did give in and rolled his eyes. "To gang up on me?"

"We're not ganging up on you, darlin'." Freckles tsked. "We're demonstrating healthy dialogue. Showing you there's nothing wrong with voicing your feelings and concerns."

"I talk about my feelings," he said, thinking of his trip to the cemetery the other day. It was the second visit he'd made to see Brie since his father's funeral, which was incredible progress considering he previously hadn't been there in over five years.

This time, his mother was the one rolling her eyes. "Perhaps you should try talking to someone who is alive, Marcus. Someone who will actually give you the advice you don't think you need."

"Ouch," Freckles said as she tossed some shredded cheese into a simmering pot. "That was harsh, Sherilee. True. But harsh. No wonder the kids get so frustrated with you."

"Oh, so now *you're* the expert on *my* children?" His mother and aunt continued their so-called healthy dialogue with such intensity they didn't seem to notice Marcus slipping out the back door.

His head was throbbing, his stomach was buzzing with hunger, and now he was working a night shift to avoid having dinner with a woman who wasn't even going to be there, anyway.

No. He wasn't avoiding Violet. He was just... Hell. He didn't know what he was doing. Marcus stared at his tired reflection in his rearview mirror. Talking to Brie had always used to make him feel better, but maybe his mom was right. There was a difference between venting and actually receiving feedback.

He'd told Violet that Brie had been a great listener, which was true. But his wife had also never talked about what was bothering her. She avoided conflict whenever possible and rarely challenged him with a differing opinion. Or told him something he hadn't wanted to hear. Being with Brie had been almost too easy at times. Too simple.

Yet nothing was simple anymore.

He'd always used to talk to Violet when they were younger, but it might be too late to go back to being friends now. Especially after their recent kisses proved that he couldn't keep his hands to himself whenever he was around her. That left his only options as fighting with her or avoiding her.

Unless she was avoiding him first.

Why wasn't she having dinner with his family

tonight? He pulled out his phone to text her before realizing he didn't have her number.

Before he could give it another thought, a call came over his handheld radio. "Be advised we have reports of an altercation taking place at Teton Ridge High School."

It could be worse, he told himself as he drove toward the highway. Nothing could top last year when the varsity basketball team was in the playoffs and Marcus had to arrest his former math teacher for streaking across the court during the fourth quarter wearing nothing but blue and gold body paint.

Then the radio crackled to life again and the dispatcher added, "Make that two altercations. And some possible vandalism. All units, please respond."

Crap. Marcus switched on his siren before advising dispatch he was en route. At least this was a public-disturbance call that didn't involve anyone from his family.

If Violet had to sit through one more antagonistic family meal with Marcus, she'd probably scream loud enough to shatter the crystal chandelier in the formal dining room of the main house. Last Friday, Connor Remington, the new owner of one of the neighboring ranches, had come to dinner and had spent the whole evening exchanging flirtatious glances with Dahlia. But the only glances Violet received across the table that night were seething glares from Marcus, who had just found out that she'd filed a motion for discovery to have his department's Breathalyzer tested for accuracy. Apparently, he didn't appreciate the insinuation that his equipment wasn't maintained properly.

Not that Violet was an entirely innocent party when it came to their petty bickering. She'd known the Breathalyzer results were likely accurate because MJ had admitted to her that he'd had quite a bit to drink before getting arrested. Still, she wouldn't be doing her job if she didn't pursue every possible avenue of defense. Besides, if she was too busy fighting with Marcus, then she didn't have time to think about how damn attractive he always looked in his sheriff's uniform.

At least that had been her initial strategy dealing with her ex-boyfriend who was making her feel all sorts of things she probably shouldn't.

Now, though, her strategy was to escape him altogether by hiding out in an overheated and overcrowded high-school gymnasium, watching a high-stakes basketball game she had absolutely zero interest in.

She couldn't even claim that she was only there hoping to find some character witnesses for MJ's case. When Roper King had become vice president, MJ had been forced to move to Washington, DC, and attend a private school, where he hadn't exactly excelled.

No, Violet had come to the game because the only

thing to do on a cold Friday night in Teton Ridge was to get a drink at Big Millie's or go to a high-school sporting event. And since she'd already been to the saloon, she'd thought she'd give basketball a try. Plus, she might run into Reed Nakamoto or Judge Calhoun at the game, which would hopefully give them the impression that she wasn't a total outsider from the big city.

It wasn't until halftime that Violet finally saw Judge Calhoun. She was behind him in line at the concession stand, and one of the parents wearing a Fling Rock High School sweatshirt dropped a tray of nachos on the judge's brand-new white high-top sneakers. Some heated words were exchanged, and the next thing Violet knew, punches were flying and she and another woman were pulling the judge from a brawl he'd caused by his overreaction to a few accidental drops of nacho cheese.

Several other parents stepped in to break up the fight, but the sound of approaching sirens could already be heard from the parking lot. The small concession area of the gym filled as the bleachers cleared and everyone came to see what was going on. There was a lot of finger-pointing over who'd thrown the first punch, and eventually Violet found her way to a nearby bench to try to wipe off the ketchup that had gotten all over her suede boot when someone lost their hot dog in the altercation.

"That's the woman who saw everything go down,

Sheriff," Violet heard a woman say, and her stomach dropped.

No, she thought to herself, refusing to look up so her eyes wouldn't confirm what her gut was already telling her. He wasn't supposed to be on duty. He was supposed to be having dinner at the Twin Kings. But when she saw the black utility boots approach her, Violet knew exactly whose legs would be attached to them.

Marcus.

"Oh, hey," Violet said a little too nonchalantly. She crumpled the red-stained napkins in her hand as she stood to meet him.

"Are you bleeding?" he asked, concern evident in his blue eyes as he searched her face for injuries. Her heart did a little flip. She liked this compassionate and nonaccusatory version of Marcus.

"No. It's just ketchup. The lady in line behind me got drenched with orange soda, so I'll consider myself lucky."

Marcus scrubbed at the lower half of his face, but not before she saw the grin he was trying to hold back. When he got his expression under control, he said, "I wish you'd told me that you were coming to the game tonight. I would've warned you to avoid the concession stand and the restrooms during halftime."

"The restrooms, too, huh?"

"Oh, yeah. People take their high-school games pretty seriously around here. Broman is currently dealing with the fight in the ladies' room, and I've got two other deputies searching for some seniors in the parking lot who were letting the air out of the tires on any car with a Fling Rock bumper sticker."

"Well, kids can pull stupid pranks when school pride is on the line."

"No, not seniors in high school. Senior citizens." Marcus bit his lower lip, probably to keep himself from joining Violet as she snorted with repressed laughter. He was the sheriff and had to maintain at least the image of being in control of an otherwise chaotic situation. "I knew I shouldn't have volunteered to cover this shift tonight."

So she'd been right, and he wasn't supposed to be on duty. Not that she was trying to keep track of his schedule. "At least you can't blame me for adding to your troubles this time."

"No, but I heard you were at the center of it. Mrs. Singh said you two broke up the fight in here."

"Who?" Violet craned her neck to see around his shoulder.

Marcus pointed to the woman who'd helped Violet hold the judge back. She was using a napkin to blot orange soda off a letterman's jacket embroidered with a beaker and the words *TRHS Science Squad.* "Mrs. Singh. The chemistry teacher."

"Oh, right." The crowd was finally dispersing, and it sounded like the second half of the game was beginning. Violet squinted at the handful of people watching them, including the scowling parent from the rival high school who'd spilled the nachos on the judge. "What happened to Judge Calhoun?"

"He should be in the back of a patrol car by now."

"No!" Violet's head jerked back to face him. "Did you seriously arrest a judge, Marcus? The one presiding over your brother's case?"

Marcus rested his hands on his duty belt. "Did he throw the first punch?"

"Yes."

"Violet, I told you that I do things by the book, and nobody in this town gets special treatment. It'll be up to the prosecutor's office to decide if they want to file charges."

What had been an almost comical situation had suddenly taken a very serious turn. A dull ache formed above Violet's temple as she considered the possible ramifications of this. "But there are only two circuit judges for the entire county. And one already recused herself from the case. If Calhoun gets removed from the bench due to judicial misconduct, it could take months for the state to appoint someone else to hear MJ's case."

Marcus rolled his shoulders dismissively. "Then it takes months."

She searched his eyes for some clue that he was hoping to delay the trial to get her to give up and return to Dallas. "I'm not leaving just because the trial date gets extended. Do you seriously think you can play nice and get along with me for that long?"

"Probably not," he admitted. "But it's out of my hands. I have to do my job, Vi. Even if the end result means prolonging all this damn sexual tension between us."

A tingle went down the back of her neck. At least he was acknowledging that he was having the same reaction to her presence as she was having to his. Really, she should be relieved that, as the sheriff, he was acting impartially and beyond reproach. Judge Calhoun really should be held to the same standards as everyone else in town.

Violet gave herself a little shake. "Fine. Do you need my witness statement?"

"Actually, do you think you can come to the station and give it? We're short staffed, and I don't want our volunteer Rod processing Calhoun's book and release all by himself."

Violet's stomach fluttered in hunger. In her efforts to avoid him at the family meal, Violet had missed out on one of Freckles's home-cooked dinners only to get herself caught up in the middle of some small-town basketball rivalry. Now she was starving, and she was going to end up spending the bulk of her evening with the very guy she'd been trying to dodge in the first place.

"Sure," she said before she could overthink it. "But I'm going to stop at Biscuit Betty's on my way there. I haven't had dinner yet, and suddenly nachos and hot dogs don't sound all that appetizing."

"Perfect. Will you grab me a chicken biscuit while you're there? Maybe a side of potato wedges?"

She tilted her head, not sure if she was quite ready to play *that* nicely yet. "Will you stop pretending to ignore me whenever we're in public?"

"I'm not ignoring you." His voice grew low and seductive as he stepped closer to her. "In fact, I'm very aware of your presence, and it takes every scrap of control I possess not to pull you into my arms and kiss you senseless every damn time I see you. But we both have opposing jobs to do, and people expect us to stay in our lanes and not get too chummy."

She stared at him in shock. "So all those times you start arguments with me, that's just for show?"

"Don't get me wrong, I like arguing with you." He smiled. "I just like kissing you more."

Marcus winked at her before walking away to interview the remaining witnesses. Violet's stomach went from rumbling to doing somersaults. If she were being honest with herself, she enjoyed kissing him more than arguing with him, as well.

But since he'd pointed out that they were supposed to be at odds, she couldn't very well bring him dinner without raising a few eyebrows. So when she stopped at Biscuit Betty's on her way to the station, she ordered enough food to feed the dispatcher, the volunteer and all the deputies on duty. Then she thought about Judge Calhoun and anyone else the Ridgecrest County Sheriff's Department might've arrested at the game and doubled her order.

When the young server gave her the total amount due, Violet smiled and said, "Sheriff King wanted you to put it all on his tab."

Chapter Nine

There was no kissing for Marcus last Friday night after the brawl at the high-school basketball game. Judge Calhoun had been booked at the station and then released, but instead of going home, the man had sat at the front desk with Rod discussing the difficulty of getting stains out of white leather sneakers. Of course, Calhoun was talking about cheese sauce, and Rod was talking about blood splatters. But at least there were no hard feelings from the judge regarding his arrest. In fact, he said he had been planning to retire soon anyway so he could fulfill his lifelong dream of attending a game at every NBA stadium in the country.

Violet delivered the chicken biscuit as promised—

as well as enough food to feed everyone who'd ever worked within a two block radius of the county buildings—and then gave her statement. But Marcus's deputies had processed five other arrests from that night, a record for his small department, and he hadn't been able to talk to her alone.

He got his bill from Biscuit Betty's the following day and nearly laughed at his ex-girlfriend's audacity. No wonder two of the people they'd brought in had jokingly asked Violet to be their attorney. He had no idea if she'd agreed to represent them, but she was certainly busy doing something, because he'd seen her at least three times that week filing documents at the courthouse.

It wasn't until the following Friday that Marcus finally got a chance to talk to Violet alone. Or at least not in front of the entire town.

His sister Tessa had been on the Junior Olympic diving team when an accident in high school had derailed her career. Agent Wyatt had secured the use of the heated indoor pool every day this week after the rec center closed to the public so that Tessa could practice diving again. Their mom and Aunt Freckles had insisted on turning this week's family dinner into a pool party and picked up a dozen pizzas from the Pepperoni Stampede in town.

"I thought you weren't going to ignore me in public anymore," Violet said to Marcus after the boys jumped into the water.

"I'm not ignoring you," he replied, still in his uniform. He'd stopped by the cabin after work to grab the boys' swimsuits but didn't want to make them wait while he changed. "I'm standing right here talking to you. In a public building."

"Technically. But you know that I'm referring to the four times you saw me at the courthouse this past week."

"I only saw you three times," he corrected before realizing he'd walked right into her trap.

One corner of her mouth turned up in a gotcha grin. "So then, why didn't you speak to me?"

"About what?" He lifted his eyebrow with a challenge of his own. "Did you want me to discuss the red lipstick you were wearing on Tuesday morning and how it's my absolute favorite color on you? Or perhaps we could've talked about the high heels you were wearing on Wednesday afternoon and how they made your legs look a million inches long? Maybe I should've complimented your windblown hair yesterday? Told you that it reminded me of the time I pulled it out of all those bobby pins at your homecoming dance right before we—"

She shoved a half-eaten slice of Hawaiian pizza into his mouth to keep him from saying anything else in front of the kids, who were splashing around in the shallow end. "Ew, I hate pineapple on pizza."

"I know." She wiped her hands on a napkin as they stood shoulder to shoulder. "So the only thing you can think of talking to me about when you see me in town is my appearance?"

Marcus finished chewing before replying, "It's not the *only* thing. But it was either that or ask you whether you had agreed to represent the same people my deputies had just arrested the previous weekend. I figured the first topic would get you all heated and aroused, and the second would get you all heated and pissed off. As much as I like to see you all hot and bothered, I figured it was best to not say anything when there were so many people around."

"You were right about the second, but not about the first. Both topics would've been condescending with zero chance of arousal."

"Really?" he asked, trying to get her to make eye contact with him. When she wouldn't, he smiled to himself. "Then why are you aroused right now?"

Violet carefully studied something off in the distance, refusing to give him so much as a side-eye. "Who says I am?"

"Your neck is all flushed, and your cheeks are getting rosy."

She swiped the back of her hand across her face, as though she could wipe away her telltale blush. "It's just warm in here. There's not much air circulation."

She'd shed her tailored suit jacket earlier, and he tilted his own head forward, purposely dropping his gaze to her breasts. Or more specifically, to her hardened nipples, which were perfectly outlined under the thin fabric of her silky white blouse. He waited for her to notice the subject of his gaze, then lowered his mouth closer to her ear and whispered, "That usually only happens when you're cold. Or when you're aroused."

She gasped and quickly crossed her arms over her chest.

"Hey, you asked." He smiled innocently then took another bite of pizza. Dang. He forgot about the pineapple. He tossed the piece into a nearby trash.

When he returned to where she was standing, she was the one smiling innocently. "For the record, I *did* agree to represent two of the people you guys arrested last week."

"So you're staying in town longer?"

"We'll see. Judge Calhoun will likely plead guilty to a lesser charge because he's anxious to avoid trial and start his retirement trip."

"Are you kidding me? You agreed to represent Calhoun?"

"Yes. But I charged him a notably high retainer. The other client I'm representing pro bono."

"Who's that?" Marcus asked, yet he had a feeling he already knew the answer.

"Rose Roosevelt."

Marcus smacked his palm to his forehead. "The woman who accosted the ref in the locker room after the game?"

"No, the concerned mom who followed the referee off the court to explain that his bad call was going to affect her son's stats, which would in turn affect his chances of earning a much-needed college scholarship."

"Violet. Rose's son plays second-string center and can't block a shot without fouling someone. Jumping on the referee's back and trying to put him in a choke hold isn't going to get the kid a college scholarship."

"Marcus, she's a single mom."

"Who committed an assault and battery."

"Allegedly," Violet corrected him.

Marcus rolled his eyes. "So are you taking the case because you feel sorry for her? Or are you doing it just to have something else to argue about with me?"

"You know—" Violet made a tsking sound before shaking her head "—arguing with you really isn't as enthralling for me as you seem to believe it is."

"Then why do you keep coming up with new ways to do it?" he asked.

"Have you ever stopped to think that maybe you're just spoiling for a fight?" she replied. But before he could reply, Jack interrupted them.

"Hey, Violet, watch this!" his son shouted before he did a cannonball into the water.

"That was great." She smiled and gave a little clap, which only encouraged Jack to want to show off more daring tricks. After each one, the boy would look to her for more applause.

"Hey, Violet." Jordan bounced up and down on his toes. "I'm trying to figure out how much lung capacity I got. Time me to see how long I can hold my breath."

Marcus and Violet stood side by side a foot away

from the pool's edge. There was a huge clock on the opposite wall, but Violet kept glancing at her wristwatch, giving Marcus the impression that she was counting down the seconds until she could politely leave.

"Do you want to come swimming with us, Violet?" Jordan asked when he emerged from the water thirty seconds later. "I watched a video on how to do CPR so I can save you if you start drowning."

"Well, that's very reassuring, Jordan, but I didn't bring a swimsuit."

Jack lifted his goggles. "You could borrow one from Aunt Tessa or Aunt Finn."

Great. Marcus could barely take his eyes off Violet when she was wearing business attire. If she put on a bathing suit, everyone in this rec center would be watching him to see his reaction. In fact, his mom and aunt were all the way on the other side of the pool, making no secret of their interest in his and Violet's current interaction. He knew she didn't have the heart to tell either of his sons no, so he spoke up. "Hey, buddy, Violet would rather hang out up here on the deck and watch you guys play."

Both boys pouted, their little shoulders sagging in defeat. Violet, who clearly wasn't used to telling children no, whipped her head in Marcus's direction. "How do you know what I'd rather do?"

He pivoted as he stepped in front of her, blocking his sons from witnessing yet another one of their disagreements. Facing her, he whispered, "Really, Vi? I'm trying to get you off the hook here."

"I don't need you to get me off any hooks, Marcus. You don't get to decide what I do, and you certainly don't get to speak on my behalf."

"Oh, come on." He put both of his hands on top of his head as he lifted his face to the ceiling in frustration. "This is a prime example of you once again finding some bogus reason to argue with me. If you had wanted to go swimming, then you clearly would've brought a bathing suit."

"Hmm. Maybe you're right." Violet took a step closer to him and slowly lifted her hands to his shoulders, letting her palms gently slide down to his chest. "And if you *hadn't* wanted to go swimming, then clearly you wouldn't have acted like such an over-bearing ass."

The next thing Marcus knew, he was falling backward with too much force to regain his balance. He heard the powerful splash before feeling the heavily chlorinated water surround him and pull him below the surface. Luckily, he was in the shallow end and was able to quickly find his footing and stand up. Unluckily, he was still dressed in his full uniform, heavy boots and duty belt full of gear, including his semiautomatic handgun and full ammo cartridges.

When he shook the water out of his ears, he could hear the twins and his niece Amelia shrieking with laughter. Or maybe that was Finn and Aunt Freckles.

The acoustics of the tiled walls caused all the howling and cheering to echo around him.

Violet remained at the edge of the pool, humor reflecting in her eyes as she stared down her nose at him, the upward tilt of her mouth smugly reassuring him that she wasn't the least bit sorry that she'd shoved him into the pool. She must've seen him lift his hand to the surface because she quickly jumped back before he could send a retaliatory spray of water in her direction. She even had the nerve to giggle at her superior reflexes before taunting him. "You missed."

"You're safe for now," Marcus promised her. "Just remember. Revenge is a dish best served cold."

Violet watched him intently, though, clearly not trusting him to not come after her for payback. He took advantage of her rapt attention by unzipping his soaked jacket and pitching it onto the deck. Next, he worked on the buttons of his uniform shirt, maintaining eye contact with Violet as he shrugged out of the waterlogged fabric and threw it on top of the jacket. He had to peel his white T-shirt off his torso and over his head before adding it to the pile, but his effort was rewarded when he saw Violet's tongue dart out as she licked her lips.

Good. Now she might understand why he'd been so reluctant to approach her in town when he already couldn't take his eyes off her. Satisfaction, and maybe a touch of pride, caused his chest muscles to stand at attention. When she jerked her eyes up to meet his, he gave her a satisfied wink.

Then, because he hadn't gone swimming with his sons since summer break, he turned to the kids and asked, "Who wants to play rocket launcher?"

"So now that Tessa's gone back to Washington, DC—" Freckles stood in front of Violet holding a small tray with a chicken-pesto sandwich, pasta salad and a slice of homemade strawberry-rhubarb pie "—Roper's old study is available for use. It might be a little more comfortable than this."

Violet moved aside some papers on the wicker patio table so Marcus's aunt could put down the tray. "Actually, I'm pretty comfortable out here in the pool house. But I'll gladly move into the study if that makes it easier for you to bring me lunch. Your pie is still the best, Freckles."

Violet had long ago given up on trying to convince the older woman that she didn't need to provide lunch every day, let alone bring it across the yard and to the pool house. It was clear that Freckles was missing her restaurant back in Idaho and truly enjoyed serving home-cooked meals to whoever she thought needed it.

"Oh, you know me, darlin'. I like the chance to come outside and get away from Sherilee bugging me in the kitchen."

"Good. Because the Wi-Fi is surprisingly strong out here, and it's much quieter away from the rest of the family. Plus, the twins already helped me decorate." Violet pointed to the numerous drawings taped to the shelves that used to hold sunscreen and beach towels, as well as the pine-cone and feather collections lining the wet bar.

"Those boys are really taken with you." Freckles plopped herself down on one of the cushioned chaise lounge chairs, extending her feet in front of her. The eighty-year-old woman was wearing five-inch wedged sandals, and Violet wanted to know how she managed to walk in those things. "You know, according to Rider, Marcus has never brought a woman home since Brie passed."

"I think we both know he didn't bring me home, either." Violet unfolded the napkin and put it in her lap. Besides, just because he hadn't brought a woman to the Twin Kings didn't mean he hadn't dated anyone since his wife's death. Not that it was any of Violet's business.

"Oh, you know what I'm talking 'bout, darlin'. Those boys lost their mama before they even knew her. Now they have you here giving them all your attention."

Violet's hands went all cold and clammy, and she nearly dropped her fork. She was the furthest thing from being a mother figure to anyone and wouldn't know how to act like one even if she'd tried. She cleared her throat. "They've grown up with Finn and Dahlia and even Sherilee taking care of them."

"Yeah, but it's different having a woman here

who isn't related to their daddy. Plus, they're smart boys. They can tell there's something going on with you and Marcus. Just like the rest of us can."

"Really? Because here I was thinking that their dad and I can't even stand to be in the same room as each other."

"Yeah. About that. The boys' birthday party is coming up. Sherilee has already blown through her secret stash of ice cream, stress-eating over the event. This is the first party she's thrown since the funeral, and a lot of townspeople will be here. Any chance you and my nephew can call a cease-fire for the day?"

Violet was gripping her sandwich so firmly a slice of chicken fell onto her lap. "Actually, I planned to fly back to Texas next week to take care of some personal business."

"You know, I always thought that was interesting. You living in Dallas."

"What do you mean? Lots of people live there."

"Sure they do. But your mama's family is from San Antonio. You went to boarding school in Washington, DC, college in California and law school in Boston." Freckles didn't miss a beat. And she'd once accused *Marcus* of creeping around the internet. "So why put down roots in Dallas?"

"I wouldn't say I put down roots exactly." Violet had a feeling the canny older woman was trying to steer this conversation somewhere, so she answered cautiously. "I have a nice condo and a good job, but

I could be a public defender anywhere. Most of my friends from school are spread all over the globe. I guess Dallas just seemed to be a nice middle ground, so to speak."

"You mean it was far enough away from your mama in Washington but also close enough in her home state that she couldn't give you too much of a hard time. I get it. I did the same thing when I wanted to get out from under my parents' thumbs." Freckles arched one orange-tinted brow. "So when are you gonna tell her you're here?"

Great. Now the rest of the King family thought Violet was afraid to confront her mother, too. She wasn't, but that didn't mean that she could simply handle the senator the same way she handled everything else. Violet sat up straighter. "I'll see my mom next Friday night, and I'll tell her then. Unfortunately, I won't be back in time for the party."

"But the twins will be heartbroken if you're not here." Freckles clutched one manicured hand dramatically to the left side of her enormous bosom, which was barely contained in a hot-pink velour tracksuit.

Violet remembered the first time Marcus's sons had invited her to their birthday party. It was the afternoon of Roper's funeral. The boys had talked nonstop about it since then, and she'd never told them that she wouldn't be attending. She sighed. "They'll be more heartbroken if I'm fighting with their dad the whole time."

"Marcus isn't going to fight with you in front of all the guests." Freckles stood up easily in her heels and walked to the door. Before she left, she added, "After all, he learned his lesson about getting mouthy with you after his little dip in the pool last week."

Ugh.

Violet had tried not to think of the incident at the rec center. Sure, she'd been impressed with how little reaction Marcus had shown after she'd shoved him into the pool. In fact, he'd been such a good sport he'd stayed in the water and played with the kids, launching them into the air as they squealed in excitement.

But not before he'd all but done a quasi-striptease for her benefit. Sure, he'd wanted to get out of his wet clothes, and nobody else at the rec center had probably thought anything of it. However, the way he'd watched Violet as he'd slowly peeled off his shirt would've been downright provocative if they hadn't had most of the King family and half the Secret Service team surrounding them.

She shook her head to clear her mind of the mental image. Instead, she tried to remember the twins' excitement at having their dad play with them and insisting that she watch them do backflips off his broad shoulders. Freckles was right. Jack and Jordan, for whatever reason, really seemed to enjoy having Violet around. It probably would break their hearts if she was a no-show for their party.

Okay, so she'd go home, attend her mom's fundraiser and then come back for their birthday. Maybe a week or so apart—truly apart and not running into each other on the ranch or in town—would give her and Marcus time to cool themselves down enough that a cease-fire wouldn't even be necessary.

"I promise to be back before the party," Violet told Jack when she walked them out to the back porch on Sunday evening after dinner.

"But what if you're not back in time?" Jordan wanted to know.

"Then I'll call you." She looked to Marcus for some backup. However, his expression was almost as skeptical as his two sons'.

"But what if you forget?" Jack asked.

"Then you can call and remind me." She knew the boys were fond of her, but when she announced at dinner that she would be going to Texas for the week, she hadn't expected them to declare that they would miss her. She was touched that they cared so much, and yet she was also sad that they clearly had their doubts about her returning. Of course, they would have separation issues given the death of their mother and, more recently, their grandfather.

"Can I call you to tell you what we did in our science lab this week?" Jordan asked.

She smiled. "Of course."

Jack squeezed her hand. "Can I call you to tell you how many laps I ran during PE?"

"I'll be waiting by my phone." She squeezed back.

"Can we call you to tell you how many times Uncle Rider says a bad word?"

"Maybe that would be better in a text message. I have a feeling he's going to say quite a few while I'm gone."

"Okay, boys." Marcus bit back a grin. "Give Violet a hug and then hop in the car. It's a school night, and we still need to hunt down Jack's missing library book that's due tomorrow."

Violet wanted to hold on to the children and never let go. But their hugs were over too soon as they raced to their father's patrol vehicle.

Marcus didn't immediately follow his sons, and Violet suddenly wondered if he was expecting a goodbye hug, as well. Instead, he asked, "So are you going to tell your mom I said hi?"

Contrary to his accusation—and Freckles's assumption—Violet had every intention of telling her mom she'd been staying in Wyoming to handle MJ's case. Telling her about Marcus would be a whole other issue.

"That might not be the first thing I say to her," Violet replied. After all, she had to be strategic about when and how the discussion happened. "But I'm sure your name will come up at some point, Marcus. The thing you have to keep in mind about my mother is that she's a United States senator. She's been shutting down her opposition on the Capitol floor at the national level and brokering trade deals at the global level since both of us were in diapers. It doesn't take courage to confront my mom—it takes skill."

He shoved his hands in his pockets, staring down at his boots. "Look, if something comes up and you can't make it back before the birthday party, that's okay. The boys will be fine."

The fact that he was already giving her permission to disappoint his children didn't sit well with her. Were his expectations of her really that low? She used her finger to lift his chin until his eyes locked on hers. "I'll see them on Saturday. You can bet on that."

On Monday, she'd spent most of the flight to Dallas going over how she was going to approach the topic with her mom. Then she'd rewritten and rehearsed her speech several more times before Friday's big event.

"You look beautiful, angel," Violet's father said when she descended the stairs at the hotel ballroom. The black-tie fundraiser was in full swing with hundreds of elegantly dressed guests enjoying the open bar and decadent appetizers, while a ten-piece orchestra played big-band dance tunes. Her dad gave her a tight squeeze, then kissed both of her cheeks. "That mountain air has been agreeing with you."

Violet narrowed her eyes. "You know."

"I had a hunch something was up when you didn't leave the funeral with me and your mom that day. That hunch grew when I realized you were only responding to my texts instead of FaceTiming with me like you normally do. Then I stopped by your office last week after my sportscast to surprise you with lunch, and your assistant filled me in."

Scanning the room, Violet saw her mother talking to a well-known socialite who was feeding bits of beef Wellington to the Pomeranian in her arms. "Did you tell Mom?"

"Do I look like a rookie playing in the minor leagues?"

She reached up and straightened her dad's bow tie. "No. You look very handsome. As usual. So, do you think she's going to overreact?"

"Not tonight. There'll be too many important donors here to keep her from batting an eye at any curveball you send her way. But don't be surprised when she calls you tomorrow to lecture you about your life choices."

"I already did my scouting report," she said, easily reverting to the familiar baseball euphemisms of her childhood. "I talked to her press secretary. Mom has a packed schedule the next two days, and then you guys fly to Geneva for that climate meeting with the United Nations."

"Smart girl." Her dad gave her a pat on the back. "You locked in your game-day strategy."

"Game-day strategy for what?" her mom asked, having escaped the socialite with the fluffy dog.

"My new case," Violet said before kissing her

mother's cheek. "Is that dress from the designer I suggested?"

Unable to resist a compliment, her mom ran a hand over the red sequins. "Yes. You were right about the color. I needed to update my style."

"I usually am right about most things, Mom." Violet smiled as the conversation began exactly as she'd planned it. But then she saw someone out of the corner of her eye and completely forgot what she was going to say next.

Congressman Davis Townsend was standing with a gray-haired couple on the other side of the dance floor, but he was staring directly at Violet. The last time Violet had seen him, Marcus had been escorting him from the Twin Kings. Crap. There was no way a kiss up like Townsend wouldn't make his way over here eventually.

Plus, her dad had now slipped away to the buffet table and she might not get another one-on-one opportunity like this tonight. She needed to explain the Twin Kings situation to her mom before the congressman brought it up. Instead, she blurted, "Did you tell Marcus's father that I had an abortion?"

"Violet," her mother admonished between clenched teeth. "Now isn't the time to discuss this."

Crap. She'd been saving that topic for later in the conversation, but now she'd have to adapt and forge ahead. "Well, we could have discussed it fourteen years ago, but you took matters into your own hands then. So now we can talk about it on my terms. I'll start. You shouldn't have lied about what happened. Even if you thought you were doing it for my own good."

"For the record, I never used the *A* word," her mom said as she smiled at someone across the room and did a finger wave. "It's not my fault the boy chose to believe what he wanted."

"Why would he believe anything else? He never got any of my letters at boot camp." Violet narrowed her eyes. "Or did you have something to do with that, as well?"

This time, her mother did gasp before quickly recovering her composure. "Of course I didn't have anything to do with that. In fact, I picked up the phone several times to call the base commander and demand that they put Marcus on the phone immediately. I almost flew out there in person to knock some sense into him for ignoring your letters like that. You think I wanted to see my only daughter suffering?"

"Well, you certainly didn't want to see us together. You were ultimately responsible for his silence afterward and didn't do anything to change that. Why didn't you ever approve of him, Mom?"

"Because no matter how well-connected his family was, I knew he was going to hold you back. He made no secret that he hated politics and desired nothing more than a small-town life. I wanted so much more for you."

It was turning into the same argument they'd had

a million times before. Violet sighed. "But I wanted *him*."

"I know you did, angel." Her mom reached out and gently stroked Violet's bare upper arm. "You don't think I remember how devastated you were? I was there. I saw what you went through. If I could've taken on that heartache for you, I would've traded spots in a second. But there was nothing I could do to ease your pain. The next time I ran into Roper King, I wasn't about to give him or his son the satisfaction of thinking you were still pining in agony for some childhood crush. So, yes, I implied that you'd handled things and moved on with your life."

"He was a lot more than a childhood crush, Mom. Marcus loved me and was just as devastated as I was."

"Then why didn't he come and see you? Why didn't he fight for you?"

"Probably the same reason I didn't fight for him," Violet admitted, her heart still heavy as she wrestled with that truth. "We were young and hurting and didn't know how to overcome the obstacle of someone who was trying to keep us apart." She looked at her mother squarely. "Just keep in mind neither one of us are children anymore."

Her mother straightened, once again schooling her expression from concerned mother to perfectly composed senator. "I know. I saw him staring at you at Roper King's funeral. He's still handsome, I'll give you that. But if I hadn't intervened back then, you'd be living on a ranch in the middle of Wyoming right now with no hope of a judicial career, let alone a political one."

Violet took a glass of champagne from the tray of a passing server. "Funny you should mention that, Mom. Because I'm currently living on a ranch in the middle of Wyoming with absolutely no intention of doing any other job than the one I'm currently doing."

For the second time of the evening, her mother gasped, and she whipped her head toward Violet. "You're kidding me."

"Senator Cortez-Hill." Davis Townsend had finally descended on them. "What a beautiful party."

"Congressman." Her mom quickly recovered with a forced smile. "Have you met my daughter, Violet?"

"We saw each other a couple of weeks ago at the Twin Kings, but we weren't formally introduced." The man's smirk suggested he wasn't as embarrassed as he should've been, which meant he was hoping to gain something by bringing up their unfortunate meeting now. "Although, you didn't look quite as... put-together in the stables that day as you do tonight."

There it was. The man was trying to establish some sort of pretense of a friendship with Violet that would get him one step closer to her very powerful mother. His mistake was in thinking that Violet would be so embarrassed by being caught in a compromising position with Marcus, she would feel resigned to play along with his little game.

"Oh, was that you?" Violet blinked innocently, enjoying the way his fake grin faltered at thinking someone didn't recognize him. "Normally, the Secret Service provides those of us living on the Twin Kings with a daily list of *authorized* guests expected to visit. I don't remember your name ever being on it. Now, if you'll excuse me, I see one of my former law-school professors over by the bar, and I wanted to consult with her on several federal trespassing statutes I'm currently researching."

Violet lifted her head victoriously, walking away just as another donor approached her mom. She'd gotten thrown off her course for a second back there, but she was leaving the fundraiser having accomplished what she'd set out to do.

Overall, her trip to Dallas had been a success. Violet had spent some time in her office updating her cocounsel on several outstanding cases. She'd watered the plants at her condo and sorted through the mail that her neighbor had been putting aside for her. She'd even had after-work drinks with a few friends from work. But most importantly, Violet had confronted her mother about interfering in her relationship with Marcus all those years ago and made it clear that she would be in Wyoming for the foreseeable future.

Now all she had to do was fly back to Twin Kings and get through a birthday party for a couple of seven-year-olds without shoving their father's head in the cake.

How hard could it be?

Chapter Ten

"My mom said she and Aunt Freckles brokered a temporary truce with you for the day," Marcus told Violet Saturday afternoon as he tried to wrestle a disposable paper tablecloth into place without tearing it.

"I believe Freckles's word was *cease-fire*," Violet said, lunging to catch the cardboard dinosaur centerpiece before it hit the ground. "Maybe you should use some tape to keep the wind from blowing stuff all over the place?"

"Or maybe we should've just had the party at the Pepperoni Stampede like we do every year?" Marcus looked up at the deceptively clear blue sky, hoping the forecasted March rainstorm wouldn't arrive a day early. "Nobody hosts a kid's birthday outdoors in Wyoming until after spring."

"The boys wanted an inflatable obstacle course and a *Jurassic Park* theme. That's kind of hard to pull off at the local pizza place." Violet used a toy brontosaurus as a paperweight to hold the flimsy centerpiece in place. "Besides, your mom needs something to focus on besides MJ's court case."

"Oh, is my mother driving you nuts?" Marcus couldn't help giving her an I-told-you-so look. "Who would've ever imagined that?"

"Mrs. King tried to invite the new judge to the party, Marcus. It's totally inappropriate."

"So is letting MJ have Kendra Broman here as his plus-one," he pointed out. "I heard you were the one pushing for that."

"They're under strict orders to stay in plain sight under the party tent at all times. Besides, there'll be at least a hundred people here watching them."

"Like that ever stopped us?" Marcus said.

Her shoulders gave a little shudder, as though a shiver of awareness had just raced down her spine. Instead of taking the bait, though, she moved on to the next table with the decorations blown into disarray. Marcus jogged over to the box of party supplies Finn had delivered earlier and found a roll of tape.

"Here," he said, passing the tape to her before holding the blue paper tablecloth steady. "Let's try your idea."

They worked together quietly for several minutes, and it felt almost…nice. By the time they got halfway through the decorations, though, Marcus couldn't stop himself from asking the question he'd been dying to know. "So how was your trip to Dallas?"

"It was productive," Violet replied, studying his face. "But what you really want to know is if I spoke to my mom. I did. She admitted that she'd purposely misled you after you got out of boot camp."

"You didn't believe me?"

"No, I did. But I still needed to confront her on it."

"Did she apologize?"

Violet crinkled her nose as she focused on untangling a plastic T. rex from the strings in the *Happy Birthday* banner. "Of course not. Nor will she. My mother will always think she acted in my best interest. But at least now she knows that I'm aware of her interference and that you and I are moving past that."

"Moving past that?" Marcus's hands stilled and his throat constricted. He had to swallow several times before he could ask, "As in getting back together?"

"I meant moving on and getting closure."

"Oh," he said, surprised at the sudden hollowness inside his rib cage. That couldn't be disappointment, could it?

Violet met his eyes across the table, her grin somewhat mischievous. "But I *might've* let her believe that we were getting back together."

His chest pinged back to life, yet he refused to sound as hopeful as he felt. "And why would you do that?"

"Because it'll serve her right to think her efforts to

keep us apart all those years ago were in vain." Violet knelt to tape a corner of the tablecloth to the leg of the folding table. She was still on her knees when she smiled up at him. "Plus, every so often, I need to remind her that she isn't in control of my life."

Oh, man, Marcus was a sucker for that smile. It was infectious, and he couldn't help but grin in response. "So let me get this straight. You're using me to piss off the senator?"

"Do you mind?"

"It depends," he said, squatting in front of her. He heard the breath catch in her throat, and he lifted his hand to push a strand of hair behind her ear. "What do I get out of this deal?"

"Hey, Dad," Jack hollered as he zipped through the open field and toward the tables at a full run. He tripped, then got back up and resumed his breakneck pace. "The inflatables are here!"

Jordan was a few paces behind his brother. "I think we should have rules for the bounce house. Like only one person at a time. So nobody gets hurt."

"Are you sure you'd rather be a doctor instead of a lawyer?" Violet asked the boy.

"Why can't I be both?" Jordan replied, causing a burst of pride in his dad.

"I'm gonna be a monster-truck driver when I grow up," Jack said, then both boys sprinted back toward the driveway.

Marcus stared at Violet as she watched his sons. Her soft expression could only be described as smitten. She sighed. "It's hard to believe they're only seven."

"Tell me about it." He jerked his thumb toward the party-rental trucks. "Anyway, I better go see about the delivery. Maybe make sure nobody brought a dunk tank. I wouldn't want you to send me into the water again."

"Are you kidding?" Violet chuckled as her eyes scanned the length of him. A current of awareness raced through him as she made her appraisal. "I never get to see you in anything other than your uniform. I plan to take a break from arguing with the sheriff today and simply enjoy watching you in your dad jeans."

"These aren't dad jeans." Marcus feigned outrage as he rose to his feet. "They're actually quite fashionable."

"I meant that they're jeans and you're in dad mode today. I'm going to sit back and appreciate both."

"In that case, I'll try to give you something worth watching." Strutting away, he did his best impression of strutting down an imaginary runway, relishing the way her laughter echoed in his ears as he moved on to the next task.

It turned out Violet didn't simply sit back during the party at all—either as a spectator or a guest. She finished decorating the tables, read over the waivers for the inflatable course before ensuring each parent signed one as soon as they arrived, helped

Freckles carry out platters of food and then took a turn as the line judge during Finn's impromptu dodgeball contest.

Marcus didn't get a single second to talk to her because there was constantly something that needed to be done. Anytime he did get a chance to slow down for a second, there was Melissa Parker trying to corner him and invite him to yet another Social Singles event. In fact, he'd just escaped her when he passed the empty bounce house and noticed one of the stakes had come out of the ground. That couldn't be good. He fixed it, then poked his head inside the safety netting and was surprised to see Violet sitting cross-legged in the corner.

"Vi?" he asked as he awkwardly climbed inside toward her. "Are you okay?"

"Yep." She held up her canvas sneaker. "This went missing during the potato-sack race. Amelia told me she saw Keegan Parker throw a bunch of shoes into the bounce house. It was so quiet in here, I figured I deserved a few minutes of downtime after getting trampled during the piñata."

"Yeah, standing in front of the rope line at the exact second the candy busts out is a rookie mistake." Marcus plopped beside her, causing Violet to bounce into him. She didn't immediately straighten so they ended up leaning against each other. Or sagging against each other, depending on who asked. "It's almost as dangerous as taking the stick away from the blindfolded kid who won't stop swinging."

"Are birthday parties always this much work?"

"Only when my children invite half the town and Finn organizes the games. As soon as that first minivan full of guests arrived, I was already cursing myself for not taking my mom up on her offer to hire a professional event planner to do everything."

"Why didn't you?"

"Because it was supposed to be a simple seventh-birthday party, and I've always wanted my kids to have as normal a childhood as they could. Unfortunately, their Gan Gan doesn't seem to have any concept of what constitutes *normal*."

Violet chuckled. She leaned her head back against the netted wall behind them, and Marcus caught a glimpse of half of her face. He did a double take, then lifted his hand to her chin. "What happened to your cheek?"

"Oh, I was going for prehistoric fairy, but the face painter ran out of glitter for the scales and went back to her car to get more supplies. The water-balloon battle broke out behind me, and I decided it was every person for themselves at that point. I made a run for it and have been hiding in here ever since."

He used his thumb to caress her jaw, which was smeared with greenish-brown face paint. "You are such a good sport. A lot of the other moms decided to hang back under the heat lamps in the tent drinking Dahlia's Irish coffees. Yet you're out playing with the kids and getting your hands—and face—dirty in the process. No wonder my sons adore you."

Something flashed in her eyes, but she quickly blinked it away. "If I'd realized cocktails and heat lamps were an option, I might've planned my day differently. But I'm not a mom, so I didn't really know what I was getting myself into."

She'd tried to make a joke out of it, but he heard the sadness in her voice and wanted to kick himself. "No, it has nothing to do with you being a mom or not. And I shouldn't have made an insensitive comparison like that. It was more of a reflection on who you are as a person. You treat the twins as though they're on the same playing field as you. You never talk down to them or make them feel as though their opinions don't matter just because they're children. But you also don't expect them to be perfect little adults all the time. They know you respect them as individuals, and that makes them want to be around you even more. What I'm trying to say is…" He paused long enough to swallow down his own emotion. "Thank you for being yourself with my children and for letting them be themselves with you."

Her lashes grew damp, and she wiped the corner of her eye. "I appreciate you telling me that. Most of the time, I feel like I'm just trying to keep up with them. They're so smart and so compassionate, and I love how everything is black and white with them. I know this is weird, but sometimes it feels as if they're the ones teaching me how to be a better version of myself."

"Well, I already like this version of you," Marcus

said as he lowered his face to hers. But before his lips could touch hers, something thumped the back of his head. It was another avalanche of footwear.

"Stop stealing all our shoes, Keegan," Jack yelled as he chased a bigger boy across the field.

"Hey, Dad, Miz Parker is looking for you again," Jordan said as he popped his head inside the bounce house. "Oh, hi, Violet. I didn't know you guys were playing in here."

"We weren't really playing, we were—" Marcus got cut off when several more kids tumbled into the bounce house and sent him and Violet careening into the air. She managed to get to her feet before Marcus did and shot him an unapologetic grin before hopping in sync with the other kids.

"Popcorn in the middle," someone cried out as the group formed a jumping circle around him. The higher they got, the more he flipped and flopped like a kernel of corn in a hot pan of oil, unable to get himself upright.

"Pop! Pop! Pop!"

Violet's smile was wide, and her voice joined the chants a bit too eagerly.

Marcus would've rolled his eyes if he wasn't already so dizzy. Yeah, she seemed to be keeping up with his sons just fine.

"How are you still standing upright?" Violet asked Freckles as she padded into the kitchen an hour after the birthday party had ended. The older woman was still buzzing around the counters, putting leftover food into storage containers and loading the dishwasher. Violet couldn't remember the last time she'd been this exhausted. How did the children have so much energy?

"Because I know how to pace myself, darlin'." Freckles handed Violet a glass of cabernet and a chocolate cupcake. "You were running around with those kiddos nonstop today. Did you even sit down once?"

She flashed back to her ten minutes alone in the bounce house with Marcus. But before she had time to give their near kiss too much thought, Uncle Rider spoke up from his slumped position on one of the kitchen chairs.

"How 'bout me? I 'bout threw out my damn back lifting dozens of little buckaroos on and off the ponies all afternoon. Or maybe I hurt it when I went down that blasted slide on the inflatable obstacle course."

"I'm surprised you could get that—" Freckles pointed a serving spoon directly at Rider's very prominent belly "—ten-pound belt buckle of yours over the rope wall."

"Figures you'd know how much this buckle weighs, considering how many times you've taken it off—"

Violet quickly interrupted Rider. "One nice thing about a small-town community is having most of the guests stay after the party to help clean up." She took a long gulp of her wine, letting the liquid relax her from the inside out.

"You can say that again." Freckles snapped a lid onto a plastic container full of smoked brisket. "Speaking of cleanup, I see you were finally able to get that face paint off."

"After quite a bit of scrubbing and a lot of hot water," Violet replied before biting into her cupcake. Freckles had given her some industrial-strength makeup remover and insisted she go take a shower while Marcus loaded all the unwrapped gifts into his SUV to take back to their cabin. She wondered if he was still at the main house or if he'd already gone home. She took another drink of wine, then said, "I saw the boys and Amelia setting up their sleeping bags in the den. Are they staying the night?"

"Yep. They were so hyped-up on sugar and overstimulation I told Marcus to leave them here for a sleepover so he could go on back to his cabin and enjoy a little bit of peace and quiet. Oh, no." Freckles frowned. "I can't believe I forgot."

Normally, the woman was all smiles and sassy comebacks, so seeing creases of concern rather than laugh lines around her mouth immediately made Violet pause. "What's wrong?"

"I just realized I forgot to send Marcus home with any food. I didn't see him eat a thing today at the party, and Lord knows what that man has in the fridge at that cabin of his. Rider, grab the keys so you can run some leftovers to him."

Rider made a grumbling sound as his hefty frame slouched even lower in his chair. "Woman, I don't think I could walk to my truck right this second, let alone climb inside it."

"Well, I can't drive in the dark with my sense of direction," Freckles replied.

"You don't seem to get lost finding *my* cabin every night," Rider mumbled before clearing his throat. "But, yeah, I guess Marcus's place is a little farther out."

Both pairs of eyes swung toward Violet, and she held up her palms. "Don't look at me. I don't know how to get there."

"Rider can draw you a map." Freckles batted her false eyelashes. "Please, darlin'. You know I'm gonna worry myself sick if one of my kiddos goes hungry."

Violet swallowed down the remainder of her wine to keep herself from pointing out that the so-called kiddo in question was a grown man who knew how to get himself to the market in town. But Freckles was the same woman who insisted on bringing a tray of food to Violet every day in the pool house whenever she worked through lunch. Plus, a small part of her wanted to see where Marcus lived.

"Fine," Violet said before stifling a yawn. "Let me go get my boots and jacket."

She had to act at least a little put out, otherwise they might get the impression that she was eager to see Marcus. When she returned to the kitchen, she picked up the very detailed map Rider had somehow managed to draw in a short amount of time, as well as a large brown paper bag loaded with enough food to feed half the cattle hands on the Twin Kings. On her way out the door, she grabbed the keys to one of the ranch trucks because there was no way she wanted anyone seeing her rental car coming or going from Marcus's place.

The sun had set over an hour ago, but even the star-filled Wyoming sky couldn't hide the fact that Marcus's cabin wasn't a cabin at all. It didn't have a single log or river rock making up its architecture like most of the other buildings on the ranch. Rather, it was a large one-story spread in a modern hacienda style with high arches, white stucco walls and a red tile roof. It reminded her of her grandfather's estate outside of San Antonio.

The front door opened before she'd even made it out of the driver's side, and the sight of Marcus standing there shirtless on his porch took her breath away.

Nope, those certainly were *not* dad jeans.

"Are the boys okay?" he asked, his eyes searching the dimly lit interior of the truck as he crossed the cold ground in his bare feet.

"Yes! Sorry to worry you. Freckles sent me to deliver some dinner. She was convinced you might starve to death if I didn't come straightaway with barbecued ribs, smoked brisket and what feels like ten pounds of corn bread."

"Well, that was very thoughtful of my aunt," Marcus said as he easily took the heavy bag from Violet, "considering she just stocked my freezer yesterday with a tray of lasagna, a tub of beef stew and at least eight chicken pot pies."

Violet squeezed her eyes shut before shaking her head. "Why do I feel like I've totally been played?"

"Because Freckles is just as crafty as my mom and twice as subtle. Especially when she gets Rider to play along with her schemes. Did you eat dinner yet?"

"I didn't even have time to eat lunch today. I'm operating on half a cupcake and a glass of wine, which probably explains why I so easily fell for your aunt and uncle's ploy to get me out here."

"Well, we wouldn't want all their strategizing to go to waste." Marcus jerked his chin toward his front door. "Come inside, and I'll share some of this potato salad with you."

Following him into his house would be a huge mistake. They could barely control themselves around each other when there were people right outside his office or the stables or even the bounce house. His place was at least a mile away from anyone accidentally stumbling in on them, offering a false sense of security from the risk of getting caught.

Which, now that she thought about it, actually made it the perfect place to finally lose control. Nobody would have to know. They could release some of their pent-up sexual tension and maybe get whatever this was out of their systems.

Violet took one step. Then another. Before she knew it, Marcus had the front door closed behind her, and the bag of food was forgotten on the floor as he pulled her into his arms. Apparently, his thoughts had been on the exact same page as hers, because he angled his mouth over hers and murmured, "Just this once."

Violet would've nodded earnestly, but he was already kissing her. Holding her face securely in place as his tongue stroked hers, encouraging her lips to open wider to accommodate him. She allowed her hands the opportunity to finally explore the bare skin of his chest and then his wide shoulders. She'd been aching to trace the ridges of his defined muscles and feel the silky dark blond hair under her fingertips, but it wasn't enough. If his body felt this good against her palms, it would feel even better against all of her.

Without breaking the kiss, she tore off her coat and went to work yanking her top higher. In her haste, one arm got stuck in her sleeve, and Marcus pulled away long enough to help her get first her sweater and then her camisole over her head. When she was standing in front of him in just her bra and her jeans, he stared appreciatively at her breasts before lifting his eyes back to hers.

"Are you sure?" he asked, his voice low and raspy.

She nodded before unclasping her bra. "But we can't let anybody find out."

His only response was to reach behind her and flip the dead bolt into the locked position. She pulled his mouth down to hers again and sighed as her aching nipples finally pressed against the hard planes of his chest. Marcus lifted her in his arms, and she wrapped her legs around his waist as he carried her through the entryway and toward what must have been the formal living room. She caught a glimpse of them in the mirror hanging over the fireplace mantel, both of them still wearing their jeans.

As he lowered her onto an oversize sectional, Violet's fingers wrestled with the button on her waistband and then her zipper. She couldn't get her pants over her hips soon enough. Marcus was undoing his fly just as eagerly but then paused. "It's been a while since I've done this. The lab results from my last physical were clear, but I don't have any protection."

They were both older and wiser this time around and knew better than to leave birth control to chance. She relaxed against the sofa cushions and said, "I've had my IUD for a few years, and I got screened when I saw my doctor in Dallas earlier this week. Just in case..."

"Just in case you couldn't keep your hands off me?" Marcus asked playfully as he finally shoved his own jeans lower. His arousal sprang forward, and Violet slid her palms down his rib cage and then to his narrow hips, pulling him closer.

"It's not my hands you need to worry about," she said breathlessly as he settled himself between her thighs.

"I know. It's that wonderful mouth of yours." He claimed her lips in another kiss as he entered her.

Violet shuddered at the familiar sensation of Marcus filling her. It had been fourteen long years since they'd done this together, but it felt as normal to her as breathing. He pulled back slightly, and she drew her knees up on either side of him, causing his next thrust to go even deeper.

Marcus groaned before setting a tentative pace. But Violet didn't want to go slowly. This ache, this coil of unsatisfied need, had been building inside of her ever since she'd seen him again. Now that her release was finally within her grasp, she wanted to race to it.

Clinging to his shoulders, she rocked her hips in a faster tempo. His breath quickened while hers came out in short pants. His arms slid under her waist, pulling her tighter against him right as she shattered through the finish line.

"You know, I can't ever remember a time when we actually took our time making love," Marcus told Violet as he lit a fire in the fireplace. He'd been so incredibly spent in her embrace that he'd remained there for nearly fifteen minutes before realizing that if they stayed like that any longer, they might catch a cold. "When we were younger, there was always such a rush because we were afraid of getting caught."

"I'm still afraid of getting caught." Violet pulled a decorative throw blanket over herself. "The last couple of times we started anything, someone in your family walked in and nearly busted us."

Marcus never bothered to use this room since it was supposed to be for formal occasions. Suddenly, though, he couldn't imagine a more formal occasion than having Violet back in his arms. And she looked so beautiful lounging there in her afterglow, he had no intention of carrying her back to his rather informal bedroom.

"Well, I can assure you that the twins won't bust us tonight. Once they fall asleep, they're out cold until the morning." The fire blazed to life behind him, instantly warming his bare backside as he turned toward her. "So we've got at least a few hours to slow things down for round three."

"Round three? Did I miss the second round?" Violet stretched, one dusky nipple popping out from under the blanket. Marcus felt himself stirring to attention already.

"No," he said before rejoining her on the sofa and pulling her onto his lap. "That round is starting right now. Then we can refuel with some dinner before we take our time."

Violet laughed throatily as she hooked one leg around his hip and lifted herself astride him. It wasn't until midnight that they finally dragged themselves to the kitchen to reheat the food they'd abandoned by the front door. Along with most of Violet's clothes.

"You're right," Violet said as she stood in front

of his open fridge. "This thing is so well stocked, I can't even find room for these leftover containers. And it's not even premade meals in here."

"I'm actually a pretty decent cook, you know."

"Since when?" Violet arched a brow.

"Since always." He grabbed their heated plates from the microwave and carried them to the living room. Violet followed with two glasses of wine.

"You never cooked for me," she said as they settled under the blanket in front of the fire.

"Because we usually only saw each other when we were on vacations with our parents," Marcus reminded her. "There were always restaurants or private chefs around."

"You didn't have a private chef here on the Twin Kings?"

"We have a cook for the ranch hands at the bunkhouse. But my dad never liked anyone but family in our kitchen. His grandma ran a moonshine operation out of Big Millie's Saloon during Prohibition and was extremely suspicious of strangers snooping around what she referred to as her *recipes*. She instituted this rule that only people with the King last name were allowed to cook in the family kitchen."

"But there were caterers at the funeral," Violet said, oblivious to the smear of barbecue sauce on her chin. "I know because I caught a ride with one to my hotel in Jackson Hole."

"Yeah, my mom pushed for caterers to be an exception when my dad first started running for office and they had to host occasional parties on the ranch. My dad did a lot of the cooking, but after he became governor, he never really had the time. And nobody wanted to eat what my mom came up with for meals."

"So you had to learn to cook for yourself?"

He nodded, swallowing a bite of corn bread. "And my siblings, when my parents were on the campaign trail. But only if we didn't feel like eating in the bunkhouse. The rule only applies to the main house."

"How did I not know that? That's a pretty big responsibility, Marcus."

He shrugged. "I'm the oldest. It comes with the big-brother role."

"Is taking care of them still your responsibility?"

"Logically, no. But old habits die hard."

They ate several more bites in silence before Violet paused and faced him. "Even MJ? Other than the time he threw up on the Ferris wheel at the county fair, I don't ever recall you having to babysit him or hang out with him at all when we were teenagers."

A familiar guilt gnawed at Marcus. "He was born when I was fourteen. I remember being mortified to tell my friends that my parents were having another baby because then everyone would know that my mom and dad were still having sex. And eww. Who wanted to admit that to their buddies? MJ was an infant, and I was starting high school. I was busy with homework and playing sports and doing all those leadership camps in summer, seeing you whenever I could get the chance. I rarely took care of him. MJ went wherever my mom went, and she and my dad were traveling a lot more for his campaigns. Us older kids stayed here with Rider, although he and Freckles were already separated by then. I joined the Marines and was gone for four years. When I came home, MJ was spending more time at the governor's mansion in Cheyenne than here in Twin Kings. After that I had my own family, and he and my folks moved to DC and, well, we just never really bonded."

"Do you think his arrest is going to help you in the bonding process?"

He sighed. "No. Maybe. All I know is that I should've been a better big brother to him back then, and I wasn't. I'm doing what I can now."

Violet studied him over the rim of her wineglass. "What if MJ doesn't want a big brother? The same way you resented having a little brother all those years ago."

"I didn't resent it, exactly." He thought about MJ bringing up the story about going on the carnival ride alone so Marcus could sit with Violet. The guilt settled in deeper. "I just had other things going on. I'm trying to make it up to him."

"Okay, think about it this way." She tucked her feet under her legs. "The first five Kings were an already-established, tight-knit group before he came along. You and MJ might've had the same parents, but you grew up under such different circumstances. He doesn't have all those shared experiences that bonded you older siblings. In a way, it's almost as though MJ was inadvertently raised as an only child. When you look at it from his viewpoint, it's not fair to suddenly insert yourself into a role that existed in name only. Especially not after he lost his father so recently."

"I lost my father, too."

"Yes. But you had thirty-two years with Roper King. MJ only had eighteen. I remember you when you were that same age, Marcus, and you would've been just as lost as your brother is now. You need to give him time and space to deal with things in his own way."

This. This is what his mom had meant when she'd said that Marcus needed someone who wouldn't just listen to him but would tell him the things he needed to hear. He'd been so focused on his own guilt for not being a better big brother to MJ, he hadn't stopped to think of what it had been like for the teen to feel as though he'd never really fit in with the rest of them.

Still. That didn't mean Marcus was going to sit back and let MJ ruin his own life. But maybe Violet was right and he'd been approaching it from the wrong angle this whole time.

"Hey." He gave her a quick kiss, then wiped the sauce off her chin. "Thank you."

"For what?"

"For making me see things from a different perspective. For challenging me."

She took his plate from him and set it beside hers

on the coffee table. Then she returned his kiss. "And here I thought *you* were the challenging one."

"I tried to be. But you've clearly already worn me down."

"I hope you're not too worn-down. I was promised a round three."

Marcus groaned before proving that he was a man of his word.

They never even made it to the bedroom before dawn slowly crept up on them. The sun shone into the wide windows of the living room, and Violet stirred in his arms, then fell right back to sleep wedged between him and the sofa cushions. After the birthday party yesterday and then all their lovemaking last night, she had to be exhausted. Marcus eased himself from the sectional without waking her and went to the kitchen to start the coffee maker before getting in the shower.

When she'd shown up at his door yesterday evening, Marcus had told himself that it would just be this one time. But now that they'd spent the night together, there was no way that he would be satisfied. Maybe the twins would want a sleepover at the main house again tonight. No, that wouldn't work. It was Sunday, which meant they had school tomorrow.

He'd call and check on them when he got out of the shower, and if his mom insisted on keeping them for the day, then maybe he could convince Violet to stay a little longer.

But when he came out of the bathroom, Violet was

already wide-awake and talking to someone on her phone. Marcus could only hear one side of the conversation, yet that didn't make him feel like any less of an eavesdropper. Especially since Violet seemed to be on the receiving end of an interrogation.

"No, Mom, I flew back to Wyoming Friday night after the fundraiser," Violet said, and Marcus's blood couldn't decide if it wanted to run hot or cold.

"I'll be staying here until after MJ's trial." Then another pause.

"Of course they have other attorneys in Wyoming. But I'm doing this as a favor to their family, which is the least I can do after you interfered in their oldest son's life all those years ago. Plus, Sherilee is trying to keep it out of the press, which I know you can relate to, considering you didn't want anyone knowing what *your* daughter was doing when she was that same age." Wow. That was both strong and logical. Good for Violet.

"Yes, Marcus is here." At this, he straightened his spine and took a few steps closer to announce his presence. But something held him back.

"He lives on the Twin Kings, so I see him quite regularly." Violet's tone was practically boastful, so maybe she really did want to get her mom all riled up. Another point for Violet.

"I don't know if we're getting back together, but—" There was a heavy sigh, which meant the senator must've interrupted her. Marcus held his breath as he waited for Violet to defend him. To defend their relationship.

Instead, Violet replied, "I know my life is in Dallas, Mom. I have no intention of throwing away my career. Speaking of careers, what time is your speech with the Girls in Technology organization?"

The subject had changed and that was it. Feeling deflated, Marcus let out the breath he didn't realize he'd been holding. Violet had been so close to telling her mother to mind her own business, but then she'd done what she always did with the senator: acknowledge the concerns without denying them and then steer the conversation to a neutral topic. Marcus almost didn't recognize this version of her, since he hadn't seen it on display since they were teens. He'd gotten too accustomed to the Violet who'd passionately argued with him about something as inconsequential as a William Shakespeare play or the suitability of pineapple as a topping for pizza.

Or maybe she wasn't fighting her mother on the issue because she was in complete agreement with the woman. Either way, Violet clearly planned to return to Texas when MJ's case was over. Marcus was no longer a naive recruit at boot camp holding on to the hope that they had a future together. They both wanted different things out of life, and that was okay.

However, there was one thing they'd never really talked about, and he wasn't quite ready to let her leave until they had.

He went to the kitchen to pour them both some

coffee, then returned to the living room to find her dressed in her clothes from the night before. He handed her a cup, then sat beside her and tried to keep his voice as bland as possible.

"Listen. Um, you mentioned something last night. About having an IUD. And I was just wondering…" He swallowed past the apprehension that threatened to cut off his words. He had to know. "Is having kids still a possibility for you? I mean physically?"

He heard the slight catch in her throat, almost a hiccup sound, and hurried to explain himself. "God, I didn't mean that to sound so intrusive. It's just that we've discussed what happened with us after the miscarriage, but we never really talked about…you know, the actual thing itself."

Violet bit her lower lip, then looked around the empty house, as though to confirm their conversation wasn't going to be overheard. Or interrupted again. "As far as I know, yes, I can still have kids. But there could be risks, and I don't know if I could handle going through that again."

He slipped his free hand into hers, pulling their joined fingers onto his lap. "Will you tell me what happened?"

It took her a few seconds, but finally she nodded. "When you left for boot camp, I thought I was only a few weeks along. At my first doctor's appointment, though, they did an ultrasound and told me I was at eleven weeks. With twins. It's probably a good thing you didn't get that initial letter at boot camp because

I was already freaking out that this was more than we'd anticipated, and I didn't want to tell my parents yet. But I didn't hear back from you, so I started thinking that maybe you were more panicked than me. I sent another letter the following week, trying to sound more upbeat and positive. By that time, I'd convinced myself that we were so blessed and were going to be amazing parents, and I'd even started thinking about decorating a nursery in some imagined home we didn't even have yet. But still no response from you."

While Marcus gently held her palm in one of his hands, his other fist tightly gripped the mug handle, wishing he could go back fourteen years ago and punch someone. "Most of my drill instructors were pretty decent, and I was so careful not to let anyone know who my father was because I didn't want them to treat me differently. But we had this one staff sergeant who was such a jerk. One of those guys who kept track of how many recruits he could make cry in a day. He figured out who I was early on. He must've been smart enough to allow all the envelopes with the name King on the return address through, because I never got suspicious that anyone was messing with my mail. They took our phones away as soon as we checked in on the base, and we never had internet access. It killed me not knowing what was going on with you, but other guys in my unit were getting breakup letters and I tried to be relieved that at least you hadn't sent me one of those.

I did manage to write you a couple of times. I'm guessing you didn't get any mail from me, either?"

Violet shook her head, then sighed. "It's not like you could've done anything about it anyway. When I got my next ultrasound at fourteen weeks, they could only hear one heartbeat. The doctor explained that since our twins were identical, they were sharing the same placenta and sometimes only one of them got enough nutrients to survive. She tried to reassure me that I could still carry the surviving baby to term but said that we'd have to do a procedure to remove the other one since it was too late in my pregnancy for my body to naturally expel it."

"Oh my God, Violet. I can't even imagine…" Marcus swallowed the knot in his throat. "I am so sorry that you had to go through that alone. I should've been there."

Her eyes were damp, but her chin jutted forward. "I'm not going to lie. That was one of several thoughts that went through my mind. 'How can I do this without Marcus?' 'How am I going to tell him that I lost one of his babies?' Then it was 'How dare he not be here to go through this with me!'"

"Aw, Violet." Marcus let go of her hand long enough to put his arm around her and pull her closer. "I know that neither one of us had planned on being parents so young. The pregnancy was a shock, but it was also thrilling. Thinking about you and our child—I didn't know it was more than one at the time—was what got me through boot camp. I wanted to have a family with you. But I would never have blamed you for the miscarriage."

"Now I know that. But at the time, I was such a mess of emotions in that exam room, the nurse had to call my mom since she was the only person listed on my emergency-contact form. I'd been such a coward for not telling my parents about the pregnancy before then. But my mom never said a word. She arrived right as they were about to take me in for surgery. At first, the procedure went as expected and I tried to console myself with the fact that we would still have one baby. But they kept me in the hospital overnight because there was too much bleeding, and by the next day, the second baby was gone. I was devastated and inconsolable, but I was also postpartum, and a heavy fog of depression set in along with everything else."

He stayed silent, letting her continue.

"That first week out of the hospital was a blur. I was just an empty shell. My mom had to hold a cup of water up to my lips to get me to drink fluids. She brushed my hair and changed my pads because even getting myself to the bathroom was an overwhelming task. Eventually, the depression lifted as my hormones evened out, but then came the denial and the anger and all those other stages of grief you hear about. The odd thing was, it was my mother who defended you. Who told me that you were probably under too much stress with boot camp and a potential military deployment. When I didn't hear back from you, well… We all know what happened after that."

He let out a deep, shuddering breath. "I know that we can't go back and change things, but…" Pausing, he dragged his hand through his still-damp hair. "Man, I wish I would've been smarter and more understanding, and not so damn stubborn."

"Me, too. We both were young, and our emotions got the better of us."

He lifted one brow. "You say that like we're not going to let our emotions get the best of us this time."

"That's because we're not, Marcus. This…" She pointed at him and then back at herself before making a circular motion at the rumpled blanket on the ground. "This is just us getting the physical stuff out of the way so that we can think clearly about everything else going on in our lives. We both have people depending on us, and we can't afford to get too caught up in what might've been."

Marcus knew better than anyone that there were no guarantees in relationships. By now he'd built enough of a wall around his heart that he wasn't going to leave his happiness up to fate. He would have to be satisfied with making the best of their time together while they had it.

Chapter Eleven

"Explain to me again why your mom and Freckles think that *all* of you need to go to Washington, DC, to get Tessa and Agent Wyatt together," Violet asked Marcus as they stood under the hot spray of the shower inside the pool house.

It was supposed to have been just one night of lovemaking. At least that's what Violet had told herself. But then one night had turned into a hot-and-steamy thirty minutes in the front seat of his patrol unit, which had led to an interesting encounter in the dusty file room at the courthouse. Now it was almost a game for Violet and Marcus to find secret locations where nobody would discover what they were up to. Her office at the pool house was usually off-limits because it was too close to the main house, and when the boys came home from school, it was the first place they looked for her. But it was still morning and Sherilee and Freckles had left the ranch for the day to talk Dahlia into what sounded like an ill-conceived plan. Romantic, Violet thought, but also very ill-conceived.

Marcus rinsed the soap off his face, then resumed his explanation. "My mom is getting the Presidential Medal of Freedom at the White House for all her charity work when she was the second lady. If the whole family isn't there, Tessa will immediately get suspicious. Even Duke is taking leave to fly in."

"How's Duke doing, by the way?" Violet switched spots with him, so she could rinse off, as well. "He seemed pretty sad when he left the ranch."

"I think something is going on with him and Tom. I tried to bring it up when he was here, but he said he couldn't talk about it."

"That's rough."

"It was," Marcus agreed. "Actually, it was kind of a punch in the gut because we've always talked to each other about everything."

"I meant that's rough for Duke." Violet squeezed the excess water out of her hair. "But sure, let's make it about another bruise to your already-fragile big-brother ego."

"I agree with you one time about one sibling and you never let me live it down." Marcus cut in front of her to block the hot water. She turned the faucet to cold then ran for her towel, leaving him to yelp as she jumped out of the spray.

"So how long are you guys going to be gone?" she asked, trying not to stare at his abs as he rubbed the dry towel over them.

"Just one night. We fly out in the morning, stay the night in DC, then bring the jet back on Sunday."

"I bet MJ will be excited to get away from the ranch for a while. Even if it's only for twenty-four hours."

"That's one of the reasons why I can't take the boys. MJ has a lot of old school buddies in Washington, and he always used to slip his Secret Service tail when he was living there. I'm going to need to keep him occupied so he can't get into any more trouble."

She noticed that Marcus said *keep him occupied*, which implied participating in an activity together rather than acting as his jailer. That was progress at least. She bent forward to wrap her wet hair in a separate towel. Someone was going to start wondering why Violet was going through so many beach towels when the outside pool was only forty degrees. When she flipped back up, she asked, "So then, who's going to watch the twins?"

Marcus tucked his chin and gave her a wide-eyed helpless stare.

Violet gulped. "Me?"

"That would be amazing, Vi," he said a bit too quickly. "Thanks so much for offering."

She narrowed her eyes. "You know full well that

wasn't an offer. I've never so much as babysat a child, let alone supervised two of them for twenty-four hours straight. At least not by myself."

"But you hang out with the boys all the time, and they love being around you. Plus, they'll be sleeping for at least nine hours of your shift. Probably."

"Shift?" Violet crossed her arms. "Am I getting paid for this?"

"I can pay you in other ways." He began kissing her neck, and she giggled before hearing a noise outside. They jumped apart, neither one of them wanting anyone to catch them. After several heart-pounding seconds of nobody knocking on the sliding glass doors, Violet finally let out a relieved breath.

"We can talk more about the details tonight," Marcus said as he pulled on his uniform pants. "I'll owe you big for this. And so will Tessa, if things work out between her and Agent Wyatt."

The rest of the afternoon, Violet vacillated between being thrilled and being nervous as hell. She was flattered that Marcus trusted her enough to leave his sons in her care. At the same time, she was seriously concerned that Marcus trusted her enough to leave his sons in her care. What was she going to do with two seven-year-olds for a whole day?

The situation got even more complicated when Marcus called her later that night to fill her in on the latest. Apparently, Dahlia's ex-husband, Micah, was going to be coming into town to stay with their daughter.

"The thing is," Marcus continued, "Dahlia's apartment above Big Millie's is only two bedrooms, and even though she and Micah get along great, she thinks it would be awkward for him to sleep at her place. Micah and Amelia are going to stay at the main house at the Twin Kings. So would you mind staying at my cabin with the boys?"

Micah Deacon was a famous musician, but Violet had never met the man. According to Dahlia, Micah was a doting father who was as active as he could be in Amelia's life, considering he lived in Nashville for work and spent a lot of time on tour with his band. It sounded like Micah could probably use some quality alone time with his daughter. Plus, Violet didn't like the idea of having a stranger witness all the babysitting mistakes she was bound to make with Jack and Jordan.

She tossed and turned all night trying not to think of all the things that could go wrong. When that failed to lessen her anxiety, she took one of her migraine pills and figured she might as well get a couple of hours of sleep before reporting for her so-called shift.

The following morning when she arrived at the cabin, Violet wished she had insisted on staying at the main house. Jack and Jordan were, of course, thrilled to see her, but Marcus was rushed and unfocused and kept rattling off last-minute instructions as he put away a box of cereal in the fridge and a gallon of milk in the pantry. She followed him from the kitchen to the front entry and then back to the kitchen when he realized he'd left his suitcase by the recycle bin.

"If you need the first-aid kit, it's in the right-side cabinet in the master bathroom," he said as they made their way to the front door. Again. "But if it's something more serious, then just drive to the hospital in Jackson. They already have both boys' insurance cards on file because we make a lot of trips there. If it's worthy of 9-1-1... Crap, I forgot Rod was covering for the dispatcher this weekend. Try not to call 9-1-1."

Violet gulped. "Is this supposed to be putting me at ease?"

"Don't worry. You guys *should* do fine." His emphasis on the word *should* wasn't any more reassuring. But he continued babbling out instructions. "Freckles stocked the fridge again, but the boys might try and talk you into going to the Pepperoni Stampede. I keep a bag of quarters in the top drawer of the mudroom for the arcade games. But don't let Jordan near the salad bar because the manager gets annoyed when he starts talking about salmonella and *E. coli* in front of the other customers. And Jack isn't allowed to use the claw machine because one time he climbed inside and...never mind. I'm supposed to be at the airfield in ten minutes. Okay, what am I forgetting?"

It suddenly occurred to her that Marcus was just as nervous about leaving his children overnight as she was about watching them. Surely, that had to be more stressful for him than anything she was going through. She threw back her shoulders with a confidence she didn't quite feel and asked, "So where should I sleep?"

"Oh." He paused. Then looked over his shoulder toward the formal living room where they'd slept the one and only time she'd been to his house. He took the small travel bag she'd packed and said, "Follow me."

They went past the dining room and then a smaller family room where the boys were sprawled out with blankets watching TV and eating cereal. An arched hallway led to what must be the bedrooms, and Marcus turned into the first doorway on the right. The room was furnished nicely, but it was also very nondescript. There were no photos, no books, no personal touches to give it the appearance of actually having been lived in. It was a guest room.

Okay. So Marcus was sticking her in a guest room. Violet wasn't sure what she'd been expecting, but her heart sank. No. She wasn't going to make a big deal out of it. It was probably better for the boys to see her sleeping in here rather than in their father's bed, anyway. How would she explain that sort of thing to them?

He set her bag on the dresser, then pulled her into his arms and gave her a deep kiss. "I really wish I could make this goodbye a little longer, but I'm already running late. Call me if you need anything."

And with that, he was gone.

Violet resisted the urge to go down the hallway to explore the rest of the bedrooms. Instead, she tentatively approached the family room, took a deep breath and asked the twins, "So what do you guys want to do today?"

There were several outlandish ideas and a few disagreements, but in the end, Violet sat down at the coffee table in the family room with a yellow legal pad and treated this discussion as she would any other settlement conference.

"Okay, so Jack's suggested activities are bungee jumping, dirt-bike racing and going to that new axe-throwing place in Jackson Hole. Jordan, your suggestions are the Discovery Center, dinosaur-bone excavating and going to the pharmacy in town to use their blood-pressure machine." Violet waited until both kids nodded in agreement before continuing. "Now, let's see which of these options are going to work best for our needs. According to the Let Loose Adventures website, you have to be fourteen to jump off the bridge over Snake River. The Discovery Center looks interesting, but it's all the way in Casper, and we'll never make it back in time to watch that superhero detective show you guys were telling me about."

It took another thirty minutes of negotiating, but they finally compromised on taking one of the four-seater ATVs—with Violet, not Jack, driving—

out exploring for caves and ancient artifacts. Jack was very impressed with her ability to do what he called *sick burnouts*, and Jordan was very excited to find a femur bone he was convinced belonged to a nineteenth-century buffalo, as well as several arrowheads. One of the boys' birthday gifts had been a pair of Nerf bows and pad-tipped arrows. So Violet set up an impromptu archery range, which was way safer than throwing axes, and held still while Jack attempted to shoot an apple off her head. On their way to dinner at the Pepperoni Stampede, they stopped by the pharmacy, and Jordan explained to her that her blood pressure was—surprisingly—in the normal range at 105 over 68.

It turned out, the only person who had sustained any sort of injury that day was Violet. And it wasn't until after she'd put the boys to bed and gone back to the kitchen to open a bottle of wine, intending to toast herself to a successful day of babysitting. A little too anxious to celebrate her victory, her thumb slipped on the condensation of the bottle, and she jabbed herself with the corkscrew.

It was a small gash, but started bleeding again every time she bumped it. Marcus had said the first-aid kit was in the master bathroom; however, Violet had been trying to avoid that particular part of the house.

It was either go get a bandage or risk having Jordan wake up and see a pile of discarded paper towels soaked with her blood. The poor boy would probably insist on giving her stitches himself. Violet steeled her spine and quietly made her way down the hallway.

When she got to the door, though, a heaviness made her stomach queasy.

The king-size bed was covered with a fluffy floral-patterned comforter and throw pillows in assorted sizes and colors. There was a silver frame on the dresser holding a different wedding photo than the one she'd seen in the main house. In this picture, Marcus and Brie were happily staring into each other's eyes. Just when Violet had gotten over feeling like an impostor babysitter this morning, she now felt like an intruder in another woman's house.

Turning to the bathroom, she quickly made her away across the plush rug, wanting to get in and out of there as soon as she could. She knelt and opened the right-side cabinet, reluctant to see any other personal items, and was relieved that the only thing on the shelf was the first-aid kit. She quickly found a bandage and wrapped it around her thumb, before deciding to grab a couple more for backup. She certainly didn't want to come back in here if she didn't have to. But when she stood up in front of the vanity mirror, she could see the reflection of the enormous walk-in closet directly behind her. The door was slightly ajar, and behind it, a row of Brie's clothes were still hanging there.

So this was the reason Marcus hadn't taken her to his bed that first night she'd spent here. And why he'd installed her in the guest room today. The master bedroom wasn't necessarily a shrine to his dead wife, but her presence could still be felt.

Violet's phone rang in her pocket, startling her. She saw Marcus's name on the screen and swallowed down her panic. There was no way he could possibly know that she'd been in the master bedroom snooping around.

No. This wasn't snooping.

It was discovery. She had known all along how much he'd loved Brie. This only served as a reminder that Violet could not allow herself to fall for a man who was no longer hers.

"Hello," Violet said, when she finally picked up. Marcus had waited for so many rings, he'd half expected the call to go to voice mail. But hearing her voice on the other end sent a wave of contentment through him.

"How're the boys?" Marcus leaned back against the pillows of his hotel bed.

"Asleep. We had a fun and busy day. I'll send you some of the pictures I took. How is everything going over there?"

"Good, actually. My mom and Freckles's plan actually worked. Grayson proposed to Tessa right there in the Rose Garden, and the media finally got the buzzworthy story they'd been waiting for. MJ and I went out to dinner, just the two of us, and then he took me to this random yoga studio on the other side of the Potomac. He said he used to go there when he wanted to get away from all the tourists and what he called *the political noise*. I had no idea he was into yoga."

"Good! I'm glad you guys are spending some time together and getting to know each other."

"I know, I know. As much as it pains me to admit it, you were right about our relationship." Marcus grinned listening to her chuckle in response. "But don't get too used to hearing me say it. Your client still has to go before the new judge."

Secretly, Marcus was hoping for another delay in the trial. The longer Violet stayed on at the Twin Kings, the more time he had to convince her to... What? Give up her life and career and move to a small town in Wyoming to be with a single dad who'd once broken her heart?

"Don't worry," she replied. "I'm looking forward to our day in court. I might even decide to call you as a character witness on your brother's behalf."

"Good try, counselor. But I think I've already proven that I'd make a terrible character witness. I'm as impartial as I can be when it comes to enforcing the law." Marcus rubbed the back of his neck, debating whether he should even risk saying his idea out loud. Why not? If it meant keeping her in town longer, it was worth a shot. He cleared his throat. "In fact, with the way my family has been behaving lately, I might even have a couple of new clients for you."

"Oh, no. What happened?"

"Do you want me to tell you as the sheriff? Or as a big brother who couldn't stop laughing when I first heard the story?"

"Definitely the big-brother version."

"You know how Dahlia has been seeing that new rancher out on the Rocking D? The one who my mom made stay for dinner a couple of Fridays ago?"

"Connor Remington?" Violet asked. "I thought I was the only one who'd figured out that there was something going on between him and your sister."

"I'm pretty sure everyone knows." Just like they all had probably figured out he and Violet were sneaking around again. "Anyway, somehow my sweet little niece Amelia convinced both Micah and Connor to rescue some stuffed animal from Jay Grover's place. When he wasn't home."

Violet's jaw dropped. "You mean to tell me that your sister's boyfriend and her ex-husband broke into someone's house? *Together?* And you're laughing about it?"

Marcus snorted. "I don't know why I think it's so funny. Dahlia is furious. Deputy Broman is annoyed because my family is indirectly involved. Again. And I'm out of town and can't do a thing about any of it."

"No, you can't," she agreed. "Which might be a good thing. You don't always have to be the fixer."

He let out an exaggerated breath. "I wish I could fix us, Vi."

There was no response, and he looked at his phone

to see if the call had been disconnected. It hadn't. "Are you there?"

"I'm here." Her voice was soft, hesitant.

Had he gone too far?

"Are you going to answer my question?" he asked.

"Was it a question? Because it sounded like a statement."

"I guess it was." He ran his hand through his hair. "What I should've said was *Do you think I can fix us?*"

"No." Her one-word response would've sent him to his knees if he wasn't already lying down. Then she continued, "I think that you alone can't do anything, Marcus. If anything needs to be fixed, it would take both of us to do it."

Okay. That sounded slightly more promising. "Do you think we should try?"

"Before I answer that, let me ask *you* a question."

"Go for it."

She paused, further increasing the suspense already zapping through his nerve endings. Then she threw him for a loop by asking, "Why didn't you ever take me to your bed?"

"What are you talking about?"

"Here at your house. We slept in the living room the first night. Then, today, you put my stuff in the guest room. Is there a reason you don't want me in your bed?"

"That *is* my bed, Vi. That's the room I use at the cabin," he said. When she didn't respond right away, he added, "Go look in the closet. All my uniforms are in there."

He could hear some background noise and then the unmistakable slide of the closet doors.

"Oh. You don't use the master bedroom?" As soon as she said the word *master*, he pictured the room in his head and wished he hadn't waited so long to go through Brie's stuff.

"No. But I know what you're thinking."

"What am I thinking, Marcus?"

"That I'm some sorry sap that can't move on from the memory of his dead wife."

"Are you?"

A blast of air expelled from his mouth. "When Brie died, it hit me hard. She was my best friend and the mother of my children. Sure, living in our house without her was overwhelming at the time. I had two toddlers and a full-time job. Moving into the main house with the rest of my family there as a sort of built-in backup helped me get through those first couple of months. I told myself that the twins and I would move back into the cabin at some point, and I even talked to Dahlia about helping me redecorate. But she'd just had Amelia and was in the middle of refurbishing Big Millie's. Eventually, months turned into years, and I became the sheriff. Looking out for everyone else took priority. A couple of winters ago, Tessa's TV network was holding a national coat drive, and I thought it would be the perfect time to finally go through Brie's clothes and give them away. Finn came to help me, and we made it halfway through the closet when I got a call from the preschool telling me that Jack got his head stuck in the opening of the puppet theater."

He heard what might've been a snort of laughter on the other end.

"Anyway, I thought Finn had stayed back to finish the job, not that it was her responsibility. It wasn't until you moved into the main house that the boys and I returned to the cabin full-time. I didn't really want the boys running in and out of the master bedroom and getting sad seeing all their mom's stuff. So I took the spare bedroom and figured I'd get around to dealing with the rest later."

"Oh."

That was it? Marcus thought. All Violet could say was *oh*?

No. He wasn't going to be the only one put on the spot in this conversation. If they were going to talk about the things standing between them, then he had a few things he wanted some clarity on, as well. "Now can I ask you a question?"

"Hold on. I'm still processing," Violet replied. Processing what? Whether she believed him or whether she thought he was holding on to way too much baggage? At least thirty more seconds went by and then she said, "Okay. Go ahead and ask."

"Does your mom still think you're moving back to Dallas when MJ's case is over?"

"I didn't tell her that I wasn't."

"You might want to consider talking to her about that," Marcus suggested.

"Why?" He could hear the dread in Violet's voice, which would've made him laugh if he wasn't worried about how she was going to react to his warning.

"Because my mom saw her at the Capital Grille today having lunch with the chairman of the foreign-affairs committee. Mom handed over her real estate agent's card and told the senator to start looking at investing in a vacation home in Jackson Hole so that she could come visit you more often."

"Crap," Violet said. Then added, "Double crap. That's my mother ringing through right now on call-waiting. I've got to do some damage control. We can talk about this tomorrow when I see you at home."

The call disconnected, and he would've been left feeling dejected that she'd referred to explaining things to her mother as *damage control*. Except he wasn't disappointed. Instead, a thrill of excitement shot through him.

She'd said *home*. Not your home. Not your family's home. Just home. As though she was already thinking of it as her own.

Chapter Twelve

"Why do our moms do this, Marcus? We're thirty-two years old, and they're still using us as pawns. Clearly, we need to stage some sort of intervention to prove once and for all that neither one of them are calling the shots on our relationship."

Violet was pacing back and forth in his office after Connor's and Micah's bail hearings. The charges were probably going to be dropped, but that didn't mean Violet was backing down as his adversary. At least not in public. But first she needed to deal with the latest development of their quarreling mothers.

"Our relationship?" he asked. "You mean the one we're currently involved in?"

"Sure. That one."

"No, Violet. I want to hear you say it."

"Don't you think we're a little too old for me to call you my boyfriend?"

"You think I'm your boyfriend," he sang. "That means you wanna be my girlfriend."

"This is so mature." Violet narrowed her eyes. "Besides, when we were on the courthouse steps a few minutes ago, I didn't hear you telling Dahlia, Connor and Micah that I was your girlfriend."

"MJ's trial starts tomorrow, and we were out in the open. Everyone expects us to stick with the routine that we can't get along. No special favors, remember? As soon as that's over, we can come clean and let everyone know."

"Do you seriously think your family doesn't already know what's going on with us?" This was the first time they'd been able to speak alone since he'd returned from Washington, and neither one had wanted to mention what was said during that emotional phone call the night before. "If your mom is giving my mom business cards for Jackson Hole real estate agents, then she knows."

"Not everyone in my family has figured out that I'm your boyfriend."

"Stop calling yourself that." Violet tried to sound disapproving, but deep down, her stomach got all fluttery when he said the word.

"Make me," he said, acting even more juvenile as he slipped his hands around her waist and pulled her closer.

Violet's attempt at a stern expression turned into a sigh as he traced his lips down her neck in a series of light kisses. A booming knock sounded on his door, and they jumped apart before Rod entered the office.

"Here's that surveillance footage a so-called anonymous source gave the DA to get those charges reduced to trespassing." The V-shaped crease between Rod's overgrown eyebrows was meant to remind Violet that he didn't approve of defense attorneys fraternizing with law-enforcement officers. The few times she'd been at the sheriff's station, the older volunteer's hawk eyes followed her wherever she went, as though he was expecting her to do something sneaky and nefarious, such as take an extra handful of M&Ms from the candy bowl on the front desk.

"Oh, thanks, Mr. D'Agostino." Violet held up a thumb drive with the video of Jay Grover breaking into his ex-wife's house the same night Micah and Connor had broken into his. Reed Nakamoto had known the case would be flimsy and had been eager to reduce the charges to trespassing well before he'd found out the alleged victim was going to make a very unreliable witness. "I brought my own copy to show the sheriff. But I'm certainly not an anonymous source. Just a concerned citizen hoping to see justice done."

"Hmph," Rod said before turning and purposely leaving the office door open. Probably so that he could keep her clearly in his sight.

"Concerned citizen?" Marcus asked. "As in a *permanent* citizen of Teton Ridge?"

Violet's stomach fluttered again, but then the sensation moved to her chest and caused a tight knot of anxiety. "I know what you're trying to get me to say, Marcus. But I'm not ready to commit to anything yet. Especially nothing as big as uprooting my life and moving to Wyoming."

An obvious cough sounded as Rod passed by the open office door on his way to the copy machine.

"Sorry about that," Marcus mumbled. "Rod thinks that every time you stop by, I'm consorting with the enemy. He's worried that you're going to use your big-city defense-attorney charm to manipulate me into doing your bidding."

"How does he know I haven't already?" Violet gave the man a friendly wave on his way back to the desk, almost enjoying feeding into his suspicions about her ulterior motives. Then she raised her voice so that Rod could hear. "So you think about what I said, Sheriff, and I'll meet you later tonight at our usual location. I'll be sure to bring that special thing you requested."

While Violet and Marcus both knew that neither of them had broken any ethical rules by being together, let him be the one to explain to his staff that their *usual location* was the main house at the Twin Kings for a family dinner. And the *special thing* he'd requested was a plum pie from Burnworth's Bakery.

Turning on her heel, she tried not to laugh at Marcus's painful groan behind her as she walked away. Too bad. He couldn't have it both ways. He couldn't call her his girlfriend in private, while at the same time want everyone else in town to think that their relationship was only professional until after the trial. He'd have to decide what he wanted—and soon.

Later that evening, Violet was sitting in the formal living room at the main house, having predinner cocktails with Tessa, Dahlia and Finn as Sherilee King shoved glossy bridal magazines under their noses. Duke had flown back to Wyoming with the family after meeting them in DC and was now trying to include Grayson, Tessa's new fiancé, and Connor, Dahlia's boyfriend, in a conversation that wasn't all about Micah's and Marcus's glory days on the high school football team.

Freckles was in the kitchen doing what she loved, and Rider was doing what he loved—taking Jack, Jordan and Amelia out for a ride on their horses. Violet tried to focus on what Sherilee was saying about bridesmaid dresses and flower arrangements, but she couldn't stop sneaking glances at Marcus. Every time their eyes met, his filled with a heat that promised what he intended to do to her once he finally got her alone.

MJ was too nervous about the trial starting tomorrow, so he'd gone back to his bedroom to be alone. And probably to call Kendra. Violet was just thinking that she should probably head back to her

room, as well, and put the final tweaks on her opening statement. But before she could make her ex-
cuses, Micah strode into the room, his eyes filled
with panic, and announced, "Hey, Rider and the kids
aren't back yet. They were expected at the stables
over thirty minutes ago."

Marcus immediately turned to Violet, and she
watched all the color drain from his face. It was
nearly dark, and his uncle's rides with the children
never lasted this long. This wasn't good.

"I'll go find them." Connor, who had once been
a tracker in the military, was the first to head to the
door.

"We'll all come," Finn said, taking off after him.

Marcus was also gone before Violet could cross
the room to him. Everyone was hurrying to the stables, and she tried not to think of the kids lost somewhere on the trail, all alone in the dark.

Mike Truong, the stable manager, was already
saddling horses, while Marcus and Grayson were
organizing who would be going on horseback and
who would be taking the ATVs. Many of the riding
trails on the ranch were too narrow for vehicles, and
Connor and Finn immediately rode off on horseback
with radios clipped to their belts.

"I'll take Dahlia to the airfield to meet the helicopter pilot," Duke said. "We'll get a searchlight up
in the air so you guys on the ground can see where
you're looking."

Even Freckles had come from the kitchen, prepared with granola bars and protein snacks to put in the emergency-kit backpacks. Sherilee did the same with bottles of water before hopping into the back seat of a departing ATV at the last minute. No way was the King matriarch going to sit back and wait patiently for her grandchildren to be found.

Violet stood there in the stables, watching helplessly as everyone sprang into action and got their job assignments. She couldn't ride a horse, and there were only so many ATVs. Only a few Secret Service agents remained on the ranch, and along with the other cattle hands, they knew the trails and the terrain way better than her. Other than being an extra set of eyes, she couldn't really offer the search team much value. But the boys were out there, possibly alone, and she needed to get to them as soon as possible. She didn't want to waste time changing into her running shoes, so she grabbed a flashlight and a radio from the table of supplies and was about to set out on foot when Marcus's voice stopped her.

"Violet," he shouted, anxiously looking around the stables for her.

Up until now, he'd been methodical and organized and completely in command as he gave everyone instructions. She imagined that, as the county sheriff, he'd participated in numerous search and rescues. But this was different. These were his own boys who were lost. How was he holding himself together?

"Over here," she said, rushing over to him.

There was the slightest flicker of panic in his eyes,

but he quickly blinked it back when he saw her. "I'm taking Micah in one of the ATVs. I need you to stay here in case the kids and Rider come back while we're all still out there."

"Oh. Okay." Logically, Violet knew that her assignment would be just as important as the others. But she hated just sitting there not doing anything. So she pushed away her own fears and forced a confident smile she didn't quite feel. "In fact, I'll probably see them before you guys, because I'm sure they're already on their way back so they can sneak in a few of Freckles's lemon bars before dinner."

He nodded and sucked in a deep breath, probably to calm his racing thoughts. Violet pulled his head down for a parting kiss then added, "Be careful. And don't worry. When they get here, I'll take care of them. I promise."

Tessa and Grayson set up a command center in the conference room attached to the bunkhouse where the Secret Service agents stayed. The radio reception was much better there, plus there were maps and whiteboards to track everybody's progress. Freckles, who had to be just as worried about Rider as she was about the children, returned to the kitchen to prep more food in case it ended up being a long night. Not that anyone could eat at a time like this. But it was probably good to have someone stationed at the house just in case they went straight there.

Violet was left alone in the stables and found herself pacing back and forth as she waited for word.

She listened intently to every transmission across the radio, her nerves becoming more frayed each time a voice came on the air to report another dead end.

No. Don't think about the word *dead*.

"Why is it taking so long?" she asked Fabio, who was hanging his head over the stall door watching her. To keep herself occupied, Violet grabbed a bucket of treats that looked like the oat clumps Marcus carried in his uniform pocket and went down the rows of stalls, feeding one to every animal who hadn't gotten to ride out for the search.

She was nearly back to Fabio's stall when it dawned on her that she was supposed to be afraid of horses. Her spirits perked up, but before she could celebrate her small victory, the radio cracked to life.

"I have the boys." Finn's announcement caused Violet to jump up in celebration, sending a few extra oat treats Fabio's way. "They were southwest of the Peabody Trail. They're tired and thirsty, but still in their saddles."

"Where's Amelia?" Micah demanded, the engine of his and Marcus's ATV revving in the background of the radio transmission.

"The boys say Rider got hurt and couldn't ride," Finn advised. "Amelia stayed to watch over him while the boys rode back to the stables to get help. But they got lost."

"Do they know where they left Amelia and Rider?" This time it was Dahlia's voice, but Violet couldn't tell if she was in the helicopter already.

"Negative," Finn said. "We'll get these two back to Violet. You guys keep looking."

Violet wanted to weep in relief that the boys were safe, but there were still two people missing. Plus, Marcus had to stay with Micah. He couldn't abandon the search for Amelia and Rider just because his own sons had been found.

"I'll take care of them," she repeated her promise from earlier to Fabio.

The engine of an ATV grew louder, and Violet ran to the stable doors. An agent was driving with one boy in the front seat and the other in the back sitting next to MJ. Even in the fading light, she could see the drying trail of tears down Jack's dirty cheeks as he frantically unbuckled and launched himself out of the vehicle and directly into Violet's arms.

Her heart went to pieces, and she wanted to hold the child close to her until she could make sure he was truly safe. But she also had to check on his brother. Jordan was the usually cautious twin, but he wasn't even unbuckling himself. He was sitting stiffly in his seat, MJ speaking quietly to him.

Freckles was hurrying across the driveway with a plate of cookies and a stack of blankets. Violet set Jack on his feet, letting Freckles wrap him in a quilt and crush him in a hug, her own sparkle-stained tears running down her face.

Violet immediately went to Jordan's side. She noticed he had a piece of fabric holding his right arm in makeshift sling. "What's wrong, Jordan?"

The boy was pale, and his lips made a grimaced line as he refused to answer.

She looked at MJ, who ran a hand through his hair before shrugging. "When we were transferring him from his horse to the ATV, his arm hit the roll bar, and he let out a scream. He wouldn't let any of us check it out. I could tell he was in a ton of pain from the bumpy ride, so I convinced him to let me use this sling to hold it in place."

"Want me to call for an ambulance?" an agent asked her.

"No," Jordan yelled, finally finding his voice. He turned pleading eyes to Violet.

Everyone was looking at her to make a decision that really wasn't hers to make. Deep down, though, she had a feeling she knew exactly what was wrong. "Let's get you out of that seat and get you something to eat. Then, you can tell me how you're feeling."

The boy squished his face in pain as Violet eased the holster seat belt away from the shoulder of his injured arm. Violet didn't think she was strong enough to lift him without jostling him even more, so MJ helped. When he was out of the ATV, MJ walked him to the bench just outside the stables and sat him down next to his brother.

Freckles went back to the main house to get some lemonade in case the boys were dehydrated. The agent explained that he had to go back and get their horses, and MJ added, "I should return to the search. Are you sure you're good here?"

"We got it." When the ATV pulled away, Violet knelt in front of Jordan. "Are you ready to tell me why you don't want anyone to look at your arm?"

Jordan sniffed, tears filling his eyes. "Uncle Rider got hurt real bad. The fire department only has one ambulance, and Uncle Rider needs it more than me."

"That's very thoughtful of you, Jordan. But you might have a pretty serious injury there yourself. Don't you think we need to get that fixed?"

He bit his lower lip, and Violet realized she had to try a different tactic. She turned to the boy's twin, who was lovingly drying Jordan's tears with a corner of the blanket.

"You're pretty good at diagnosing stuff, Jack. What do you think is wrong?"

Jack, who never paid attention to any of the medical documentaries his twin watched, shrugged. "Maybe he sprained his wrist?"

"It's not my wrist. It's a sub-cromal pinge-oment," Jordan corrected.

Violet had absolutely no idea what that was, but it sounded serious. And painful. She'd promised Marcus that she'd take care of his sons, and that was exactly what she was going to do. "How about if instead of calling an ambulance, I drive you to the hospital? Your dad can meet us there after they find Rider and make sure he's in good hands."

The boy tried to shrug but winced in pain. Violet held her breath, not wanting to push his decision. "Okay, I guess."

Aunt Freckles was returning with two insulated cups and a couple of bottles of water tucked into her apron pockets.

"All right, then. Aunt Freckles, can you please load up the snacks and the blankets in the car for us?" Violet forced her voice into a calmness she didn't feel. "We're just going to go on a little drive over to the hospital and let the doctors take a peek at Jordan's sub pingement situation."

"I don't need an ambulance," Jordan insisted to the older woman, as though she hadn't been listening in on the radio this whole time and knew full well that Rider was in trouble.

"Of course you don't, darlin'." Freckles smiled her wide grin, her bright lipstick proving to be much longer lasting against tears than her smeared mascara.

"You'll like the CT-scan machine, Jord," Jack eagerly told his twin as Violet pulled onto the main highway. Jack then rattled off all the emergency-room procedures that he'd experienced in the past five years. Instead of being distracted, though, Jordan's little face grew even more pale as he listened in terror.

Violet pushed her foot harder on the gas and prayed she was making the right choice.

Chapter Thirteen

Marcus knew this emergency room almost as well as he knew the Ridgecrest County Courthouse. The desk nurse greeted him and, before he could ask, said, "They're in room 107."

"Thanks, Cathy," he replied, striding down the hall.

When he got to 107, the door was open, and the curtain partition was pushed aside. Violet was sitting in a chair beside the bed, showing Jordan a video on her phone. Pausing a second, he watched them without saying anything. He let the wave of relief crash through him and sent up a silent prayer of thanks that they were all okay.

"Dad!" Jack paused from spinning in circles on the doctor's stool. "It wasn't me this time."

"So I heard." Marcus had found out over the radio that his sons were safe, but it wasn't the same as seeing them with his own eyes. He squeezed Jack to him before turning to look at the hospital bed. Not wanting to cause any discomfort to Jordan, Marcus had to settle for ruffling his hair. "How's the patient doing?"

"Sorry I got hurt, Dad. Is Uncle Rider okay?" Of course Jordan would be more concerned about his dad's feelings and his uncle's condition than his own.

"Don't be sorry, buddy. Accidents happen. Uncle Rider is in surgery right now, but he should be fine. Amelia is fine, too. She's with Aunt Dahlia and everyone else in the lobby, waiting to hear from the surgeon. But I'm more worried about you. What's going on in here?"

Jordan looked at the digital machine beside him. "My blood pressure is in the normal range. Pulse and oxygen are fine. They already did an MRI, and we have to wait for the results."

"In fact, the doctor should've been here a while ago." Violet stood. "Maybe I should go down the hall and find her."

"Hey." Marcus took several steps toward the foot of the bed and grabbed Violet's hand before she could leave. He lowered his voice. "MJ said he could tell it was bad, but Jordan wouldn't say anything. Thank you for taking charge."

"Of course." Violet squeezed his fingers in response, but she made a subtle side-eye look toward the boys, as though she was warning Marcus that they had an audience.

They locked eyes for several seconds, and then Jordan asked, "Are you guys gonna kiss?"

Violet immediately tried to pull away, but Marcus wouldn't release her hand. He maintained eye contact with her while asking his sons, "Why? Do you want us to?"

"Yes!" Both of the boys cheered, but Jack did so with more energy and crashed his spinning stool into the blood-pressure machine.

He lifted his brows at Violet. "They want us to kiss."

"How about we just shake instead?" They were already holding hands, so Violet pumped her arm dramatically.

"No!" the boys chorused. Jordan even giggled.

"We could compromise with a hug?" Marcus suggested, pulling Violet into his arms. God, she felt good. After everything he'd been through tonight, he didn't know how much he'd needed to hold her until she was pressed against him. Apparently, she'd needed a hug just as badly, because she wrapped her own arms around his neck and let her head fall to his shoulder.

"Uh, excuse me, Mrs. King?" A young doctor that Marcus didn't recognize stood in the doorway holding a clipboard. Violet pulled away from his embrace and looked around the room in confusion before finally realizing the newcomer was speaking to her. "I'm Dr. Yu, and I just got your son's MRI scans from the radiology department. Is now a good time for me to come in?"

"Oh, I'm not... He's not my..." Violet started, but Jordan prevented her from saying anything else.

"Is it a sub-cromal pinge-oment?"

The doctor tilted her head to the side. "How do you know what subacromial impingement is?"

Violet finally managed a reply. "He does a lot of medical research."

"Well, you're close. It's actually a dislocation. Do you know what that is?"

"Yes, but I didn't hear a popping sound," Jordan replied. "Shouldn't I have heard a popping sound?"

"Not always." The doctor turned to Violet. "So how did the injury happen?"

"Oh." Violet waited for Marcus to take the lead on speaking to the doctor, but he'd only just arrived and still wasn't sure what exactly had happened. Dr. Yu looked expectantly at Violet. "Uh, he and his brother were riding on their horses, and the trail was getting dark. They had to go under a low-hanging branch, and Jordan was worried Jack wouldn't see it. So he reached to push it out of the way, and his sleeve got caught. The horse kept going, and his arm got jerked backward."

"Ouch," Dr. Yu said, and Marcus winced in agreement. "I know the physician's assistant already did a cursory eval, but do you mind if I examine him?"

The doctor continued to direct most of her attention

to either Jordan or Violet, who she clearly assumed was the mother of the twins. Marcus would've been slightly insulted that his role as the father had been dismissed in favor of the mother if he hadn't been enjoying watching Violet easily answer the questions.

"Okay, Dad." Dr. Yu finally spoke to Marcus. "I'm going to need you to sit behind Jordan and help him stay in position like this."

"Mom—" Dr. Yu said to Violet, and at this point nobody corrected her "—I'm going to need you to hold Jordan's good hand in yours so he can squeeze it real tight. Now, I'm going to simply rotate your arm and move everything back into place on the count of three."

"Wait. Can I do it?" Jack asked.

"No!" Marcus, Dr. Yu and Jordan all yelled at the same time.

"Maybe I should take Jack out to—" Violet started, but Jordan interrupted.

His eyes were wide, and his small fingers were digging into her hand. "Please stay with me."

"Of course I'll stay with—"

Pop!

Dr. Yu had taken advantage of the distraction, and Jordan barely made a yelp.

"Was that it?" the boy asked.

"Yep. All done. You did great." The doctor again looked at Violet. "He's going to need to keep it elevated and iced. Do you have children's ibuprofen at home?"

"We can stop at the pharmacy and get some," she replied easily.

"Does he play any sports?"

"He's supposed to start baseball next week."

"You'll have to tell his coach that he can participate in the running drills, but no throwing for at least four weeks."

"Got it," Violet said, then looked at Marcus. "Hear that, Coach? No throwing for four weeks."

The doctor finally glanced at Marcus, and he wanted to tell her that he was also her patient's parent, not just the coach. But with the exception of being the muscle to hold Jordan in place, all the questions and directions were given to Violet. Which was really for the best because Marcus was too emotionally drained to remember all the instructions.

"He'll have to wear a sling for a few days. Do you need a note for school?"

"Any documentation you could give us would be great," Violet said, always thinking of the legalities.

"That didn't take as long as last time when I got my cast," Jack said when the doctor finally left. "Can we get some ice cream on the way home?"

"Sure," Violet said without even consulting Marcus. For a woman who'd been reluctant to babysit for a few hours, she was certainly warming up to the motherly role she'd been thrust into.

Cathy, the desk nurse, at least gave Marcus one parental duty. He got to sign the discharge paperwork.

The four of them left the emergency room and

stopped in the hospital lobby to check in with the rest of the family. Duke saw them coming and signaled Marcus and Violet over to talk, while Jordan showed off his new sling to everyone else.

"Rider's out of surgery, but they're going to keep him in ICU."

"ICU?" Marcus shuddered. Connor had found Rider and Amelia first, but Marcus and Micah had arrived soon after. Rider had still been pretty lucid when they'd called for medical transport.

Duke nodded. "He broke a rib, and it punctured one of his lungs. Freckles is back there now with him. The surgeon said the prognosis is good, but I didn't want to say anything in front of your kids because I know Jordan would worry."

"You're a good uncle," Marcus said, then pulled his brother in for a fierce hug. His second hug of the evening. "I know I usually don't say this, but I'm glad you're in town."

"Why? Because I'm the only one in the family with a pilot's license and could provide aerial support during the search?"

"No, because Kendra Broman just came in the door, and someone needs to make sure her daddy doesn't come in here looking for MJ."

"Big brother isn't going to stick around and keep watch on everyone?" Duke asked, and Violet snorted. "This is certainly unexpected."

"I'm taking the rest of the night off. I need a few hours alone with my family to focus on what I almost lost." Marcus wrapped his arm around Violet's waist and pulled her against his side. "Come on, boys. We're heading back to our cabin."

Violet should've been in her room at the main house planning for her opening statement at the trial tomorrow. Instead, she was at Marcus's house kissing a very sleepy Jordan good-night. Jack had fallen asleep in the truck on the way home with his half-eaten ice-cream cone in his hand, and Marcus was trying to get his chocolate-stained shirt off without waking him.

When she and Marcus left the room and shut off the hallway light, he asked, "Beer or wine?"

"Definitely wine."

He went into the kitchen, and she collapsed on the living-room sofa, thinking over everything that had happened that night. When he returned with her glass, she asked, "Why did you let the doctor think that I was Jordan's mom?"

"Because you were acting like his mom."

"I wasn't trying to be," she insisted, not wanting Marcus to think she was angling to take the place of his children's mother. She wouldn't have even known how to fill that role.

"I know. I meant you were doing all the things that parents normally do in those situations. My brain was still on overload from earlier, so I was grateful one of us could properly function. You were great at comforting him and making decisions and advocating for him."

"Well, he was doing a pretty good job advocating for himself. Man, that boy knows his medical terminology."

Marcus chuckled, then took a sip of his beer. "He also knows that he can count on you. He could've easily told Finn or MJ about his arm, but he waited and told you. Not that he didn't trust his aunt and uncle to take care of him. But because he knew that you would listen to his concerns and not override him or tell him he was silly for not wanting to call for an ambulance. I told you before that my boys not only adore you, they respect you."

Violet knew the conversation would have to take place sooner or later. She couldn't let the twins think that she was going to continue being in their lives if she had even the slightest doubt that things might not work out with their father.

She took a deep breath and faced him. "You told me that one of the reasons you married Brie was because she was so easy to get along with. But Marcus, I'm not her, and I'm never going to be her."

"Have I ever made you feel as though you needed to be? As though I didn't want you to be completely yourself?"

"The girl I used to be, or the woman I am now? Because I've changed a lot since then."

"Like you're more argumentative? Believe me, I've noticed."

"Do you know how I got this way?" she asked.

His mouth lowered into a frown. "Because I hurt you."

"Yes and no. It's important that you understand that even if we get back together, even if we try to move past all the hurt we once caused each other," she paused so that he would know that she, too, was taking some responsibility for their breakup, "there are going to be times when we still won't agree."

He lifted his knee onto the cushions to better face her. "Then help me to understand where you're coming from."

"We both know that my mother is overbearing and controlling and—" Violet exhaled "—frankly, a lot like *your* mother. Except you grew up with other siblings, who taught you how to argue, how to fight back. I had the desire, but I didn't have the training or the courage. Even back then, there was a part of me that knew I shouldn't have given up so easily. That I should have fought harder for you. Or at least fought harder to confront you. But I was young and hurt, and before I knew it, you were gone. I convinced myself that you might not be worth fighting for, but that I was. In law school, I finally found my voice. I learned how to negotiate, how to persuade and, more importantly, how to argue. And I was good at it. Distinguished law firms recruited me. The district attorney told me I could have my choice of assignments. My mom had arranged for me to clerk with the Supreme Court. You know what I chose, though?"

"To represent the people who you thought needed you most?"

"Well, that was a small part of it. But mostly I became a public defender because those were the hardest cases to win. I needed the challenge. I needed the fight because I had spent too much of my life not fighting for the things I believed in."

He picked up her hand. "Did you believe in us?"

"Back then?" She only paused to take a breath. "One hundred percent."

"What about now?" he asked.

"Right now?"

"Yes, Violet Cortez-Hill. Do you believe that we can figure out a way to fight for each other this time?"

"What are you saying, Marcus?" She didn't want anything to be said in the heat of passion or in jest. They both needed to lay all their cards out and talk about their expectations.

He cupped her cheek in his hand. "At one time in my life, I thought I wanted things to be easy. I don't regret my marriage to Brie because she gave me what I needed at the time. Truthfully, we gave each other what we needed. Plus, she gave me my children. But now I need something else in my life. I need you, Violet. My boys need you. Hell, my whole family needs you. I know that things won't be perfect and that we will have our ups and downs. I wouldn't expect anything less from you. You bring out the best in me, and you challenge me to be the kind of man that I want my sons to be. I loved the girl you once were, but I love the woman you've become even more."

Her heart filled with a lightness, and her mind was spinning. Marcus loved her. He wanted her in his life. Normally, she knew all the right things to say. But right now, all she could manage was "I love you, too."

"Then stay here," he said, before picking her up and carrying her to his bedroom. She had a feeling he meant stay in Wyoming, not just in his bed. And as he shut the door behind them, she realized there was nowhere else she'd rather be.

Except preparing for trial tomorrow. Ugh. They'd just had an intense, adrenaline-fueled night, topped by an emotionally healing conversation about their future, and Violet was going to have to leave to get ready to oppose Marcus in court in the morning. Well, not Marcus exactly. Just the deputy who worked for him and the county prosecutor.

When Marcus started kissing her, though, Violet decided that she could probably stay one more hour. Maybe two.

Before dawn the following morning, Marcus was thinking about what he was going to cook Violet for breakfast when a pounding knock came from his front door. If something had happened to Rider in the middle of the night, one of his family members would've called.

"I'll go see who it is," he told Violet when she stirred in his arms. "But I'm not going to keep it a secret that you're here."

Last night, she'd told him she loved him. This morning, the boys would wake up and see she'd spent the night. After the trial ended, everyone would know that they were together, and they could stop all this sneaking around.

Turned out, there was no need to pretend otherwise. When Marcus opened the door, MJ was on the other side and strode inside. "Is Violet awake? I need to talk to her."

"Is everything okay?" Violet asked, coming down the hall in the sweater she'd been wearing last night—inside out—and a pair of Marcus's boxer shorts. Her hair was in a messy ponytail, and her face was filled with concern. "Is it Rider?"

"Oh, um, sorry. Rider is good. He was already awake and asking Freckles to sneak some biscuits and gravy into the hospital for him. The surgeon is moving him out of the intensive care unit later this morning. But that's not why I'm here. I want to plead guilty today."

"Whoa," Violet said, not so subtly jerking her chin toward Marcus. "This might be a conversation that needs to take place somewhere else to maintain attorney–client privilege."

"I can go get some coffee started," Marcus offered, but MJ cut him off.

"No. I want you to hear this. You were right. I needed to grow up and start taking responsibility for my actions. Dad had always steered me in the right direction, and I used to sit back and let him. I know that sounds like a cry for attention, and maybe it was. But the more I acted like I needed guidance, the more Dad gave me. Then, right after my high-school graduation, Dad seemed distracted. You guys were all busy with your own lives when he first got sick, but I knew something was up with his health before then. I put off college last fall because I wanted to stay close to him. I thought that maybe if he thought I needed him badly enough, he'd fight whatever was wrong with him and stick around. When he died, though, I started thinking that maybe I should've been the one to fix him, rather than the other way around."

Sounded like Marcus wasn't the only one in the family who thought he needed to fix things. But he let MJ continue.

"I was angry and I was emotional and I was stupid. I shouldn't have gotten drunk after the funeral, and I shouldn't have punched Deputy Broman. Dad would've wanted me to accept the consequences of my actions, and I'm doing him a big disservice and causing everyone else in the family a bunch of grief by drawing out this trial any longer than it needs to be."

Neither Marcus nor Violet said anything, and MJ

released a big breath. "Well, now that I got that off my chest, I think I'll go get that coffee started. I bet you guys will need it for the rest of this conversation."

Marcus whispered to Violet, "Shouldn't you be giving him some sort of lawyerly advice right now?"

Violet whispered back, "I think he could use some brotherly advice more."

"Right." Marcus nodded and started toward the kitchen.

Violet caught up to him and grabbed his arm. "Except not so much advice as more of a listening ear. Just listen to his feelings, and let me handle the legal stuff."

When they arrived in the kitchen, MJ was pulling a box of sugary cereal out of the pantry. "Sweet. Mom never lets me keep Sugar Loops at the main house."

"So what happened to make you change your mind about pleading guilty?" Marcus asked, then grabbed three bowls out of the cupboard. They might all supposedly be grown-ups now, but nobody said no to Sugar Loops.

"You know when you took that yoga class with me in Arlington?"

"*Took* the class?" Violet brought the milk container to the table. "Marcus, you said you went there, but you never told me you actually did yoga."

"You want me to show you my planks?" He flexed his arms.

"Ew, gross." MJ set the box down so he could plug his ears. "You guys sound like Uncle Rider and Aunt Freckles."

"No, we don't!" Marcus shuddered, then shook his head. "Anyway, you started thinking about changing your plea when we were in DC?"

"Yeah. You were asking me about my electives in high school, and I told you about that biomedical science class. You said it sounded pretty interesting. So I started doing a little bit of research, but there's no way I could go to school for all the years it would take to be a doctor. Then last night when Jordan got hurt, I made him that sling, and it helped. Agent Franks and I made it back to where Rider was just before the medical evac team got there, and I got to ride in the helicopter with them. Man, I watched them save Rider's life, and I thought, hey, I could do this, too. I stayed up talking to Kendra at the hospital, and she convinced me I should become a medic. One of the guys on the flight last night told me that he was in the Army Reserve and that EMTs can pretty much get any job they want if they have a combat background. I have to figure out if the military will take me with a criminal record, though."

"Have you met our mother?" Marcus asked. "She has half of the joint chiefs of staff on her speed dial."

"I want to go about it the right way, though," MJ said, which made Marcus even more proud. "I don't want any special favors because I'm a King."

Violet finally spoke up. "Now this is where I come

in with the legal advice." She explained that misdemeanors could often get expunged from the record after time was served. She thought she could get Reed Nakamoto to agree to twelve months of probation, and if MJ successfully completed that, she could file a motion to expunge. After that, the recruiter's office would have to decide whether or not they'd be willing to accept MJ, but who were any of them kidding? Sherilee King would make some phone calls whether any of them wanted her to or not.

By the end of the day, Violet had gotten MJ only six months of probation—with credit for house arrest the past three months he'd been confined to the Twin Kings—she'd picked up the twins from school and she'd stopped by the Pepperoni Stampede to pick up dinner for the four of them.

"Day one and you're already setting the bar pretty high for this girlfriend gig," Marcus said when he opened the pizza box. "Wait. Did you get pineapples on purpose?"

"Maybe," she replied with a sly grin, then yelped when he started chasing her around the kitchen table. "I told you I wasn't going to make things too easy for you."

He changed directions at the last minute and caught her in his arms. She was now laughing breathlessly, and the boys started chanting, "Kiss her! Kiss her!"

But she took matters into her own hands and

kissed him. The boys cheered, and she whispered, "I love you, Marcus King."

His heart felt as though it was going to explode. When the boys heard the opening song to their favorite movie, they took the pizza box into the family room, leaving Marcus and Violet in the kitchen.

"Do you love me enough to stay together even when we live so far apart?"

"The main house isn't all that far," she replied. "Not even a whole mile."

"I meant when you go back to Texas," he said, trying not to hold his breath. "To your career and your life."

"As long as there's a courthouse nearby, my career can be anywhere I want it to be, Marcus. And since you and the boys are in Wyoming, then I guess my life will be here, as well."

"Are you serious?" He grinned, his wildest dreams coming true before his eyes. "You're staying here at the Twin Kings with us?"

"Yes. But on one condition."

"Name it," Marcus said.

"We hire a wedding planner. There's no way I'm running interference between our mothers when they start trying to get the upper hand on reception venues and invite lists."

His laughter echoed in the kitchen. "Is that a proposal, Miss Cortez-Hill?" he asked. "Are you asking me to be your husband?"

"No, it's the preliminary stages of a pending negotiation. We can wait until after the boys go to bed before you deliver your counteroffer."

"No counteroffer," he replied. "I accept. I'm not letting you get away ever again."

Epilogue

"I don't know why you can't get married at the First Congregation of Teton Ridge like everyone else in the family," Sherilee said to Marcus after most of the guests had left. The immediate King family was still sitting around several large tables at Big Millie's, which had been closed tonight so that Tessa and Grayson could hold their wedding rehearsal dinner there, much to Sherilee's chagrin. "You could still have your reception in Texas at a later date if it's so important to Senator Cortez-Hill."

"I got this," Violet whispered, then patted Marcus's knee before turning to his mom. "Mrs. King, my mother is already heartbroken that I'm moving to Wyoming full-time to open my own law practice.

The least we can do is compromise by following *my* family's tradition and have the ceremony at St. Thomas's in San Antonio. Look on the bright side, though. Think of how crazy Aunt Freckles is going to drive my mom when it comes to planning the reception dinner."

Sherilee seemed to mull the idea over. "I might pay to see that. But I'll talk to our church secretary about their open dates. Just in case."

Marcus pressed his smiling mouth against Violet's forehead. "Good try, counselor. You can't win every case."

"I didn't get married at the First Congregation." Dahlia raised her hand from behind the bar. She and Connor had enjoyed a very small, outdoor ceremony at his ranch, the Rocking D.

"Not this time, you didn't," Finn mumbled from her stool where she was nursing a melting margarita.

"Don't be jealous that your twin has got you beat two times over when it comes to finding great guys," Micah said.

"*One* great guy," Finn corrected, then turned to Connor who was helping his wife wash glasses behind the bar. "You're a saint for putting up with Dahlia's ex-husband, Con."

"Someday you'll have your chance to walk down the aisle, too, Finn." Micah was one of the few people who could really get under the tough cowgirl's skin. "As soon as you can find someone who wants to put up with your sassy attitude."

Tessa held up her hands in a time-out sign. "Can we please have at least one night with no major family arguments?"

"Nope."

"No way."

"Yeah, right." A chorus around the bar.

"Keep in mind, Mom," Marcus said, his voice raised as he slung an arm around his younger brother, "MJ is going to be my best man, and it'll be easier for him to attend the wedding after he gets out of boot camp if we get married in Texas."

The heavy oak door opened, and all eyes turned toward the entrance.

"Sorry we're late," Duke said as he and Tom shrugged out of their coats. Tom was wearing his dress blues, and Duke was still in his flight suit. But at least they were together.

Amelia, Dahlia's daughter who often asked more questions than Jack and Jordan combined, yelled across the room, "Hey, Uncle Duke and Uncle Tom. Do you guys have your baby yet?"

There were several gasps as everyone's heads pivoted from Amelia to Duke to Tom and then back to Amelia again. Finally, Duke smiled and put his arm around his husband.

"So you guys might've noticed that we haven't really been ourselves lately. For a while now, Tom and I have been looking into adoption. We had gone through the whole background process and were hopeful a couple of times, but then things would fall through at the last minute. It was pretty heart-crushing, and we were about ready to throw in the towel on the whole idea of ever becoming parents. But…"

"But?" Sherilee was clasping her hands together hopefully. It was no secret that she wanted as many grandchildren as possible.

"But then someone came through with the incredibly selfless offer to be our surrogate and, well, there's going to be a new addition to the family in six months."

Their mother squealed and danced around in a circle with whoops of happiness. Everyone else joined in with hugs of congratulations, and Dahlia popped the cork from a bottle of champagne.

"Wait!" Sherilee yelled over the noise. "You haven't told us anything about this surrogate. Who is she? Where does she live? What's her vitamin regimen? Does she do Pilates? I'm going to need the name of her obstetrician and her nutritionist."

"Why don't you ask her yourself?" Duke said, then nodded to where Finn was sitting quietly at the bar, apparently drinking lemonade out of her margarita glass.

"You… You're… Wow…" Micah stuttered, putting into words what everyone else in the room was feeling. Completely stunned.

"It's not like I had anything else going on, anyway," Finn snapped at him. Then she pushed herself off the bar stool. "Besides, I couldn't let my other siblings get all the attention."

There was more cheering and more champagne and more hugs.

Violet wrapped her arm around Marcus's waist and whispered in his ear, "Maybe we should wait to make our announcement. I don't want to take away from Duke and Tom's special moment."

Marcus lovingly placed a hand on her belly. "You are going to be the most beautiful bride, and I promise that I am going to be the most amazing father to our children."

Violet lifted her chin toward where Jack and Jordan were playing swords with the pool cues. "You already are."

* * * * *

*Catch up with the rest of the King family
in Christy Jeffries's new miniseries,
Twin Kings Ranch*

Tessa's story
What Happens at the Ranch…

and

Dahlia's story
Making Room for the Rancher

*Available now
Wherever Harlequin books and ebooks are sold.*

COMING NEXT MONTH FROM

H HARLEQUIN

SPECIAL EDITION

#2851 FOR HIS DAUGHTER'S SAKE
Montana Mavericks: The Real Cowboys of Bronco Heights
by Stella Bagwell

Sweet Callie Sheldrick disarms single dad Tyler Abernathy in ways he can't explain, but the widowed rancher is in no position for courting, and he won't ask Callie to take on another woman's child. The kindest thing he can do is to walk away. Yet doing the "right thing" might end up breaking all three of their hearts...

#2852 THE HORSE TRAINER'S SECRET
Return to the Double C • by Allison Leigh

When Megan Forrester finds herself pregnant, she resolves to raise the baby herself. But when Nick Ventura becomes the architect on a ramshackle Wyoming ranch Megan's helping friends turn into a home, that resolve soon weakens. After all, Nick's the total package—gorgeous, capable and persistent. Not to mention the father of her child! If only she could tell him...

#2853 THE CHEF'S SURPRISE BABY
Match Made in Haven • by Brenda Harlen

A family emergency whisks Erin Napper away before chef Kyle Landry can figure out if they've stirred up more than a one-night stand. Almost a year later, Erin confesses her secret to Kyle: their baby! But the marriage of convenience he proposes? Out of the question. Because settling for a loveless relationship would be like forgetting the most important ingredient of all.

#2854 THEIR TEXAS TRIPLETS
Lockharts Lost & Found • by Cathy Gillen Thacker

Cooper Maitland's nieces were left at the ranch for him, but this cowboy isn't equipped to take on three infants on his own. Jillian Lockhart owes Coop, so she'll help him look after the triplets for now—but recklessly falling in love would be repeating past mistakes. As they care for the girls together, can their guarded hearts open enough to become a family?

#2855 THEIR RANCHER PROTECTOR
Texas Cowboys & K-9s • by Sasha Summers

Skylar Davis is grateful to have her late husband's dog. But the struggling widow can barely keep her three daughters fed, much less a hungry canine. Kyle Mitchell was her husband's best friend and he can't stop himself from rescuing them. But will his exposed secrets ruin any chance they have at building a family?

#2856 ACCIDENTAL HOMECOMING
The Stirling Ranch • by Sabrina York

Danny Diem's life is upended when he inherits a small-town ranch. But learning he has a daughter in need of lifesaving surgery is his biggest shock yet. He'd never gotten over his ex Lizzie Michaels. But her loving strength for their little girl makes him wonder if he's ready to embrace the role he's always run from: *father*.

YOU CAN FIND MORE INFORMATION ON UPCOMING HARLEQUIN TITLES, FREE EXCERPTS AND MORE AT HARLEQUIN.COM.

HSECNM0721

SPECIAL EXCERPT FROM

H HARLEQUIN
SPECIAL EDITION

*Skylar Davis is grateful to have her late husband's dog.
But the struggling widow can barely keep her three
daughters fed, much less a hungry canine. Kyle Mitchell
was her husband's best friend and he can't stop himself
from rescuing them. But will his exposed secrets ruin
any chance they have at building a family?*

Read on for a sneak peek at
Their Rancher Protector,
*the latest book in the Texas Cowboys & K-9s miniseries
by USA TODAY bestselling author Sasha Summers!*

"Even the strongest people need a break now and then. It's not a sign of being weak—it's part of being human," he murmured against her temple. "As far as I'm concerned, you're a badass."

She shook her head but didn't say anything.

"Look at your girls," he insisted. "You put those smiles on their faces. You found a way to keep them entertained and positive and with enough imagination to turn that leaning wooden shack into a playhouse—"

"Hey," she interrupted, peering up at him with red-rimmed eyes.

"I was teasing." He smiled. "You're missing the point here."

HSEEXP0721

"Oh?" She didn't seem fazed by the fact that she was still holding on to him—or that there was barely any space between them.

But he was. And it had him reeling. The moment her gaze met his, the tightness and pressure in his chest gave way. And having Skylar in his arms, soft and warm and all woman, was something he hadn't prepared himself for.

Focus. Not on the unnerving reaction Skylar was causing, but on being here for Skylar and the girls. *Focus on honoring Chad's last request.* Chad—who'd expected him to take care of the family he'd left behind, not get blindsided and want more than he should. How could he not? Skylar was a strong, beautiful woman who had his heart thumping in a way he didn't recognize.

"Thank you, again." Her gaze swept over his face before she rose on tiptoe and kissed his cheek. "You're a good man, Kyle Mitchell."

Don't miss
Their Rancher Protector *by Sasha Summers,*
available August 2021 wherever
Harlequin Special Edition books and ebooks are sold.

Harlequin.com

HSEEXP0721

Get 4 FREE REWARDS!

We'll send you 2 FREE Books plus 2 FREE Mystery Gifts.

Harlequin Special Edition books relate to finding comfort and strength in the support of loved ones and enjoying the journey no matter what life throws your way.

FREE Value Over $20

YES! Please send me 2 FREE Harlequin Special Edition novels and my 2 FREE gifts (gifts are worth about $10 retail). After receiving them, if I don't wish to receive any more books, I can return the shipping statement marked "cancel." If I don't cancel, I will receive 6 brand-new novels every month and be billed just $4.99 per book in the U.S. or $5.74 per book in Canada. That's a savings of at least 12% off the cover price! It's quite a bargain! Shipping and handling is just 50¢ per book in the U.S. and $1.25 per book in Canada.* I understand that accepting the 2 free books and gifts places me under no obligation to buy anything. I can always return a shipment and cancel at any time. The free books and gifts are mine to keep no matter what I decide.

235/335 HDN GNMP

Name (please print)

Address   Apt. #

City   State/Province   Zip/Postal Code

Email: Please check this box ☐ if you would like to receive newsletters and promotional emails from Harlequin Enterprises ULC and its affiliates. You can unsubscribe anytime.

Mail to the **Harlequin Reader Service:**
IN U.S.A.: P.O. Box 1341, Buffalo, NY 14240-8531
IN CANADA: P.O. Box 603, Fort Erie, Ontario L2A 5X3

Want to try 2 free books from another series? Call 1-800-873-8635 or visit www.ReaderService.com.

*Terms and prices subject to change without notice. Prices do not include sales taxes, which will be charged (if applicable) based on your state or country of residence. Canadian residents will be charged applicable taxes. Offer not valid in Quebec. This offer is limited to one order per household. Books received may not be as shown. Not valid for current subscribers to Harlequin Special Edition books. All orders subject to approval. Credit or debit balances in a customer's account(s) may be offset by any other outstanding balance owed by or to the customer. Please allow 4 to 6 weeks for delivery. Offer available while quantities last.

Your Privacy—Your information is being collected by Harlequin Enterprises ULC, operating as Harlequin Reader Service. For a complete summary of the information we collect, how we use this information and to whom it is disclosed, please visit our privacy notice located at corporate.harlequin.com/privacy-notice. From time to time we may also exchange your personal information with reputable third parties. If you wish to opt out of this sharing of your personal information, please visit readerservice.com/consumerschoice or call 1-800-873-8635. **Notice to California Residents**—Under California law, you have specific rights to control and access your data. For more information on these rights and how to exercise them, visit corporate.harlequin.com/california-privacy.

HSE21R

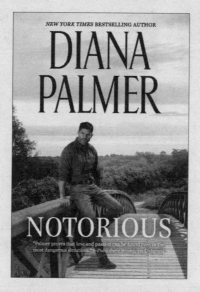

Love Harlequin romance?

DISCOVER.

Be the first to find out about promotions,
news and exclusive content!

f Facebook.com/HarlequinBooks

y Twitter.com/HarlequinBooks

O Instagram.com/HarlequinBooks

P Pinterest.com/HarlequinBooks

ReaderService.com

EXPLORE.

Sign up for the Harlequin e-newsletter and
download a free book from any series at
TryHarlequin.com

CONNECT.

Join our Harlequin community to
share your thoughts and connect
with other romance readers!
Facebook.com/groups/HarlequinConnection